The Interview

Virginia Gray

The Interview

Virginia Gray

This is a work of fiction. Any resemblance to actual persons, living or dead, is purely coincidental.

The Interview

Copyright © 2016 by Virginia Gray
ISBN: 978-0-9905236-4-2
eISBN: 978-0-9905236-3-5

First Edition January 2016

Library of Congress Cataloging data is
available upon request.

Contents

For Mom

I

Demons and Lattes

I believe my skill set is perfectly aligned with this company's needs—*whatever they are*," I recited, staring at my vague image in the foggy bathroom mirror. I squared my shoulders. "I'm top of my class at a top school and thus, therefore, and furthermore, only interested in working for a top computer company. No, too may 'tops'—and 'furthermores'. I know! You should hire me because I'm a frigging rock star!"

After finishing my epic air-guitar solo, I bowed humbly to the sold-out stadium of screaming fans. A squiggle of matted, brown seaweed escaped my terrycloth turban, splatting soundly on my forehead. Cross-eyed, I watched a water droplet meander down my nose.

Gathering my sundry bathroom items, I padded down the hallway, leaving a trail of puddles and bullshit on the slippery linoleum. "Tell you about myself? Well, I'm a Scorpio, I like kittens and puppies, and I swim the English Channel twice a year—naked. Oh, and when I'm not doling out gruel to starving children in Africa, I moonlight as an astrophysicist."

I shivered uncontrollably as I

entered my dorm room. Though my oversized sweatshirt engulfed me, it was scant protection from the chilled air. At such an expensive school, being forced to live in a refrigerator was thoroughly ridiculous. I shook out my hair, and after assaulting it with a vengeful brush, took up my circuit on the well-worn carpet, the list of standard interview questions once again in my hand.

"Where do I see myself in five years? Lounging at your desk, of course. I will take over the entire technology industry in ten. I will *own* your ass!"

"Yeah, they'll hire you on the spot with that one," Lexi said, yawning like a pampered cat. "Now shut the fuck up. The *Sigma Pi*s are rolling out four kegs tonight, and I need my pre-party nap." My roommate's slim skillset staunchly centered around drinking beer and cussing like a sailor—though, I actually didn't know any sailors, so that was simply a best guess. She offered me her back and pulled the covers over her head.

Rolling my eyes, I left, shutting the door quite soundly. What did she care about interviewing? She was busy majoring in English Literature—something completely useless, where the chances of getting a job right out of college were, like, one in ten trillion. She could afford to party; her parents had money and connections. I had me.

Drifting sightlessly to the science and technology building, I took up my pacing in its small library. With eyes mated to computer screens, no one noticed, no one cared. I'd spent the last four years preparing for this.

I was ready. But so were thousands of other almost-graduates—all competing for the same few slots out there. I thought about my past and my need for a real and splendid future. Life had not been kind to me. I was cosmically owed.

The package arrived a few days before spring break. Wrapped in brilliant, floral-patterned paper, it very simply screamed, "Mom!" Graduation was two months away. *Why so early?* Surreptitiously, a card peeked from its nest of green packing peanuts. It would detonate when opened; an explosion of well-meaning drivel and thorough disappointment.

A knock on the door rescued me from my swirl of emotions.

"Hi," he said to the floor, raking his fingers through his disheveled hair. Unable to decide whether "long and scruffy" or "neat and businesslike" would land him an orgasmic programming job, Ben's current style basically suggested "confusion". I raised a brow. "I was wondering if...coffee?"

"I'm running through my interview questions right now."

"I could quiz you!" Again with the hair, wiping too long bangs from his hopeful eyes. "My treat," he added. His smile was a failed attempt at "lopsided and cute". Heaving a heavy sigh, I surrendered to pity.

I followed his lanky form down the hall. He slumped when he walked—so uncomfortable in his skin, as if his very bones were trying to hide. One day, if he filled out and straightened to his full height, he might be considered attractive—*if.* He pushed open the doors and we plunged into the bitter whispers of winter. March was only spring in the South.

When we reached the coffee shop counter, my faithful friend, staunch companion, and always lab partner ordered his usual latte and bought a banana muffin for us to share.

"Caramel macchiato, venti, skim, extra-shot, extra-hot, extra-whip, sugar-free," I recited, all perky, when it was my turn. The barista glared vengefully at me and then worked very hard to appear aloof as she squirted steam into sputtering milk.

I am truly unable to describe to you how much I hate this person.

She'd been my nemesis since freshman year physics lab, when she'd batted her eyes at the hapless teaching assistant, tossed her bouncy blond hair over one shoulder, flicked a manicured nail in our direction, and said, "Don't waste your time with *those* people."—'*those* people' meaning the remaining entirety of the class—"We're the only ones that really matter." This statement was followed by copious giggling by her tablemates. Interestingly, that's exactly what he did: helped them with extreme prejudice throughout the semester. *Brainless sack of water and hormones.* It was the only *B* I'd gotten in four years, and I blamed her solely.

"Just ignore her," Ben had suggested the beginning of sophomore year as we slurped that rich, creamy, wonderfulness known simply as latte.

Sage, but impossible advice, for you see, Brittney was majoring in economics and minoring in computer science, which meant, annually, our collective course schedules overlapped by, oh...sixty-two percent. And while she demonstrated only mediocre intelligence, I noted with unwavering resentment that her looks performed miraculous feats in the classroom.

"You're not blond enough," I'd been informed last year.

"I'm a flipping brunette!"

"Men like blondes. Dye your hair." This from Lexi, the purple wonder.

Though I lived on the ragged edge of financial ruin, my one guilty pleasure was coffee—the delicious, foamy, syrupy, flavored kind; it was my once a week indulgence. But three days after returning from Christmas break my junior year, that special, deeply personal, almost spiritual ritual had come to a screeching halt.

On January sixteenth, nearing popsicle-stage, I'd staggered into the student union's coffee shop. I remember the date perfectly, not because the Pluto-like temperature had set an all-time record low, but because *she* was perched behind the counter like a heavily-mascaraed, ample-breasted, yellow bird, surrounded by plates of cinnamon-topped muffins and raisin scones.

Open-jawed, I watched our advanced business statistics professor smile salaciously as he shoved a large tip in her jar. My eyes dropped to my less than ample breasts, obscured by five layers of thermal outerwear. With sagging shoulders, I hunched over like Charlie Brown and slipped away, left to drink stale, artificially-creamed coffee for the rest of the semester.

Unlike the glamorous ambiance Brittney enjoyed, my place of employment afforded me slightly different surroundings: sticky countertops, spent napkins, globs of dried ketchup, and grumpy customers. A cinnamon-topped muffin had never crossed its threshold, unless smuggled in by me, and a scone? *Pah!*

Located in a slightly sketchy part of this small college town, I worked at a dated mom and pop restaurant—excuse me, "café", for that is what they called it, ya know, like Burger Hut *Café* sounded *so* much more sophisticated than just Burger

Hut. My slave-like duties offered me one small measure of perverse pleasure: the knowledge that Brittney would surely perish here.

She could never hope to handle the drunken, after-party crowd that perennially rushed in just before closing, half destroying the place in the process. Unable to leave until the kitchen was semi-spotless, the floors mopped, and the bathrooms cleaned, *she* would certainly be fired within her first week for sheer laziness.

On my most desperate nights, imagining her crying as blisters calloused her palms and fingers was what kept me going—strengthened me, even. But in the end, disregarding my secondary motivations and desperate need for money, my job taught me how to work hard. And for that I would be forever grateful.

This past summer, I'd chosen to remain in Illinois rather than travel home; a blessed freedom from the Southern chains binding my youth. There would be no hiding from those who'd manipulated me with heaping piles of faux charm, no hours of aim-less driving to avoid returning home before my parents fell asleep, no tears. In fact, from this distance, I could very easily imagine a future where North Carolina would no longer be called my home. Those were, quite frankly, the best three months of my life.

During rare moments of spare time that summer, I'd contemplated my existence—thought about the creation that was me, of who I was and what I wanted from life. The epiphany came one afternoon as I sat on the shore of Lake Michigan, listening to the raucous squawks of bandit gulls: success! I'd been hell-bent on graduating with honors since the day I stepped foot on this renowned campus, and at present, there was little chance I would fail. But I suddenly realized my focus had been shortsighted.

With less than a year to go before being mercilessly thrust into the real world, I needed to look beyond Northwestern's boundaries to a future with possibilities as grand and wide as the mighty expanse of water stretching before me. To me, success meant never having to limp home. Success meant never being beholden to anyone again. Success meant a financial freedom that would provide me with excesses—a beautiful apart-ment, fine clothing, a dazzling car. Success meant my thorough transformation into the very picture of professionalism. Success meant finding a job!

I'd dusted the fine pebbles from my shorts, trekked back to my stuffy dorm room, and fired up my computer. It was that very day that I began the search for long-term employment. It was also the day I decided that no one would ever stand between Susan Wade and what she wanted again. And at that very moment, Susan Wade wanted a latte, dammit. A *grande* latte!

Prepared to rain hellfire and damnation down on Brittney Cox's pretty head, I stormed into the coffee shop only to find a friendly face that did not belong to *her*. When I inquired about the witch, I was politely informed that she'd gone home for the summer. Of course she had! She'd gone home to her probably loving family, who surely heaped presents and most likely a shiny new convertible upon her golden crown. But come fall, things would change for her. This over-indulged, spoiled brat would be rudely introduced to the new and very much improved me. I trudged into work that evening with a new and determined sense of mission.

To my immense pleasure, senior year had transformed Brittney into an overly-taxed, overly-dramatic creature, whose life was one coffee trauma after another. Every order, no matter how simple, was invariably met with a contemptuous groan, as if pouring a cup of caffeinated froth might possibly end her world.

Fairly regularly possessed by a demon, after extensive research, I'd created a running list of challenges to torment her. Last time, I'd ordered a *tall, half-caff, soy latte at 147 degrees*. I'd nearly charred my tongue, but her expression and the wiping of her brow had been completely worth it. Next time I was thinking: *grande, quad, nonfat, one-pump, no-whip, mocha*. In all honesty, I had no idea what half that stuff really meant, but the more tiny boxes on the cup she had to check off, the deeper my satisfaction.

Her despairing attitude worked well for tips, but it infuriated me. She had no idea how lucky she was, and perhaps—okay, I was absolutely trying to punish her for taking such a glamorous job for granted. Her pathetic attempts at sympathy and meaningless gestures of helplessness would be met with contempt at

Burger Hut. Taking a sip of her latest latte travesty, I sat back in my chair and smirked as she let out another little moan.

After running through my entire list of interview questions twice, Ben casually said, "I was thinking, maybe we could go out to dinner or something."

"Like a date?" I asked, slightly appalled.

"Well, kinda. I mean, yeah."

"I'm sorry Ben, but I don't have time for a relationship right now. I won't even live in this state after graduation—*please, God!* And neither will you."

He dropped his eyes to his cup and industriously fashioned creamy swirls with his tiny red straw. He'd been working on this, I realized belatedly.

After an uncomfortable stretch of silence, he said, "Well, there's, like, until then." His oddly desperate eyes met mine.

"No. Thank you, but no."

"We don't have to go out." Pink crept up his neck.

"I'm not sleeping with you, either," I said, grimacing.

White instantly replaced pink, and he stammered, "I didn't mean—I wasn't—"

"You did, you were, and I won't." I hopped up. "Thanks for the coffee. See you in lab."

"Wait, Susan! I—" I fled the richly-scented room before he finished.

Had I led him on in some way? Lab partners and mattress partners were not the same thing. I wrestled with this burning question all the way back to my dorm. The wind had picked up, and puffs of frozen smoke escaped my probably blue lips. Class would be awkward from now on. I flopped onto my bed and stared at the ceiling. Life was rapidly changing. I rolled on my side, considering sleep, but one glance at my desk clock had me rocketing to the closet. *Crap!* I couldn't be late.

After donning my grease-stained apron, I reached for my purse and promptly tripped over that damned box. I gave it my best scornful glare. *Why had she sent it* now?

"Reporting for duty, Mr. Bellman."

"Susan, how are you this fine

evening?" I looked through the grimy window at the grimy weather.

"Um, fine, I guess. How are you?" He was in a chipper mood—rarely a good thing.

"How's that job search coming? We've got high hopes for you!"

"It's going just great, thanks." I smiled brightly to hide my distress.

I'd applied to an armful of companies, hoping that some would nibble at my shiny, fresh, almost just-out-of-college bait. To date, that number had been zero. Though the first several rejections had left a bitter residue, my heart was unshakably set on *The Big Three*: huge multinational corporations that towered like mountains over all other computer companies. These were truly the only ones that mattered to me. If I could squeeze a toe in the door of even one of them—an interview, a chance to plead my case, well, that would be everything!

"I know you love this job, so tomorrow, how would you like to work second shift, too? We're short a waitress."

"Um..." I replied, weighing my lack of time versus my desperate need for cash.

"I was just telling Margie this morning how lucky we are to have an employee like you. I said, 'Susan's a gal we can count on, no matter what'," he bellowed too jovially.

Unfortunately for me, I was incredibly dependable and really couldn't afford to lose this job. I had bills to pay and needed to eat occasionally. Plus, there was that whole coffee addiction thing to consider.

Smiling tightly, I counted the seconds until the other shoe dropped.

"And while we're at it, let's pen you in for the rest of the week, eh? Emily just quit."

I exhaled audibly. "Okay, Mr. Bellman."

"That's my girl." He patted my back, and then whispered, "I'll pay you time and a half, but don't mention it to Margie—she'll have my hide!" He belted out a walrus laugh and waved as he left for the evening. *Yes!*

Confectioner's sugar sifted onto my head and shoulders as I hurried to class the next morning. At least last night's wind had exhausted itself.

Shaking out my coat, I found a seat near the back of the lecture hall. I rolled my eyes at the guy beside me, continuing the ruse that global economics was boring. Everyone else seemed to think so, but secretly, I found the course material fascinating—all that money amassing, dispersing, redistributing. It made my head swim.

By the time class let out, it had stopped snowing, and the clouds, in all their drab glory, seemed brighter, as if the sun truly slumbered somewhere up there. That naked golden orb had shamelessly danced across the sky where I grew up; the one thing in life that comforted me. I entered the small classroom feeling hopeful.

"Hi Ben," I chirped, dumping my laden backpack on the desk.

"Susan," he replied curtly. The thwarted lover treatment. *Seriously?* We'd been friends since freshman year. He knew me, who I was, what I wanted—*and didn't want*. Why was he playing the romance card now?

We said little during lecture. He took notes zealously, and I ignored him right back. As soon as class let out, I packed up hastily and set about what had recently become my solemn ritual: mail check.

Delivery was variable, so I pilgrimaged to the campus post office twice daily, hoping for news. As with every other day for the last two weeks—the exception, that nasty note from my bank on Tuesday—my P.O. Box stared empty and unblinking. I slammed its little lid shut.

"Nothing?"

I whirled around. "Oh, are we speaking again?"

"Yeah, I guess." He stared mournfully into his equally empty black hole then back at me. "So, why do you think we haven't heard anything, yet?"

"It'll happen. We'll be offered so many amazing jobs we won't even know which to choose." It was a lie, of course, or at least a pipedream, but we both needed to believe it.

"Well, I guess I can move back home for a while," he said, shrugging. "Work part time somewhere, ya know, until my big break comes." He smiled weakly, but I shuddered at the thought. Undoubtedly, my parents would be thrilled to have me home, but in that stagnant Southern air, I would surely suffocate.

I sighed mightily. "We'll get jobs. We just have to."

"Are you working tonight?"

"As always."

"Maybe I'll stop by."

"Knock yourself out." He was wasting his time with me. My heart had been deeply scarred, and I was in no hurry to score it further. My mind traveled to ancient tragedies as I turned away. I couldn't afford to let anyone in, maybe ever again.

"Are you ever gonna open that damn box?" Lexi snapped, shucking out of her fluffy designer parka, her purple hair dripping melted snow in a ring around her feet.

"Eventually."

"What's your problem?" she hissed, her silver nose ring flashing.

"What's yours?" I spouted, completely confused.

"It's just, if my parents sent *me* something..." She focused too hard on the difficult task of removing her chunky, designer boots.

My roommate for two years, I'd never met her parents. Of course, I would totally die if she met mine—not that they'd cross the Mason-Dixon Line unless absolutely necessary, but hers...and the money they spent. Almost weekly, she received packages from one New York boutique after another, boxes spilling over with beautiful clothing, shoes, purses, accessories. Granted, she typically dumped the lot on her closet floor, but I attributed that to her general ungratefulness and sheer lack of style.

"I mean—well, your mom wrapped it herself and everything," she continued. "And sometimes she bakes you cookies and crap. I just think that's really cool."

"Yeah, but your mom—"

"My mom doesn't give a shit about me," she growled. "She only gives a shit about the way I look!" She promptly threw her boots against the wall and stormed barefoot from the room.

Okay...

Glancing at the festive wrapping and curly bows, I frowned. *Maybe tomorrow.*

2

Jersey Sucks!

Days blew by, as did a ferocious late-season storm. Though it clawed at me, I flew like a winged pixie back to my dorm. "I got a letter!" I sang, twirling around the room, twirling around Lexi. I ripped open the envelope and read the glorious invitation.

"That's in Jersey, right?" Lexi asked, peering over my shoulder. She'd been paying attention. That surprised me.

"Yes!" I spewed merrily.

"Jersey sucks."

"It's one of *The Big Three*! Don't you see? It's my ticket to freedom. ComSync's a *Fortune 500* company. I'll get bonuses and benefits and a fantastic salary. I'll travel. I'll be important!"

Lexi rolled her eyes and snorted. "Yeah, whatever."

"Can't you be happy for me? This is a big deal!"

"Okay, sure. I'm happy," she replied flatly.

With a huff, I left in search of someone who could properly celebrate with me. I found him on the sidewalk in front of the library.

"ComSync? That's fantastic!" Ben shouted, picking me up and turning me in a circle.

"I know, right?!"

"They'll make you an offer as soon as they meet you," he said with an exuberant nod.

"I doubt that. But what if they did? I'd totally accept without thinking twice!"

"I totally would, too. I'm so jealous."

"You'll get your letter soon! I know it. Any company would be lucky to have you. You're like, the next Steve Jobs." He pulled me into his arms again, hugging me tightly and for a bit too long. "Um...Ben?" I said, my voice muffled by layers of down-filled winter wear. "You can let go now."

The heels of my tan shoes were modest. Modest suggested calm confidence and the flavor of propriety. Though I'd worn them to my high school graduation, I'd kept them in very good shape. They looked nice—dated, perhaps, but nice. My blouse was cream-colored crepe with a conservative neckline. It had been on winter clearance at Belk's department store—not that they actually suffer winter in North Carolina. More like, it frosts most nights in January. The rest of my scant Christmas money had ransomed my suit from Talbots' layaway.

Understated, the cut was highly conservative, but certainly feminine—what with it being bright pink and all. My mother, who worked part time at the small clothing store, had snagged it right off the mannequin. "It's the latest!" she'd gushed, and then promptly put down a five-dollar payment and locked it in storage.

After viewing too many hours of C-SPAN for a political science project, I'd reconciled my mixed feelings about the shade. Congresswomen wore vibrantly colored suits—the better to be seen. I needed that exposure, that visibility. I needed companies to know that only I could really get the job done. Me.

"That outfit looks stupid."

"No, it doesn't," I replied to my snotty roommate—the one wearing the... "Are those legit army boots?"

"Cool, huh?"

I noted a suspicious stain on the right toe. "That's probably blood, you know."

Her eyes lit, and she smiled evilly. "Even cooler!" She then glanced at the brightly wrapped box, pressed her lips together tightly, and glared at me. I shrugged nonchalantly and continued ironing my *non-stupid-looking* outfit.

After she exited in her usual fashion, I carefully retuned the ensemble to its hanger and fitted my makeshift garment bag over it. The black shone fearsome in the fluorescent light, a testament to Hefty's finest. I fingered the pearls before putting them back in their hiding place. They weren't real, of course, and Lexi would never steal them, but they'd been my grandmother's, and they meant a great deal to me. She'd been the first of many tragedies to come—casualties in the war against tobacco.

Glancing at the box, the first fingers of guilt grazed my skin. *Maybe tomorrow.*

U

ComSync wasn't housed in the nicest part of New Jersey, and though my car was a literal piece of shit, I was somewhat concerned it might be stolen as I pulled into a questionable-looking McDonald's. I scurried inside, suit in tow. Bypassing the line of coffee-deprived patrons, I raced to the bathroom to change. Having driven all night, my sweats were wrinkled, worn and smelled a little ripe. And though my eyes danced with caffeine and adrenaline, I carefully blotted their pale purple rings with concealer.

"I can do this," I murmured to the smudged glass before fleeing the scene. With my worldly possessions stuffed in a trash bag, I looked like a well-dressed homeless person crossing a litter-riddled lot.

Admission into the parking deck came only after pleading my case and literally shoving the interview invitation in the attendant's face. Once inside the gray, fortress-like complex, a disinterested receptionist casually eyed me, smirked, and then slid a visitor's badge across the counter. I gushed appreciation and asked for directions. She nodded to the ancient security guard, whose withered finger then pointed towards a bank of elevators.

Filled with eager anticipation and a great sense of wonder that I was actually standing on ComSync's hallowed ground, I squared my shoulders and tried to look important. The elevator doors opened, and I was thrust into a beehive of activity.

Phones droned in urgent undulation, employees buzzed from one desk to the next, lighting on some, leaving papers, like pollen, on others. It was mystical.

"Your credentials are very impressive. Double-majoring in computer science and business was a smart move. We like smart people." A manager in acquisitions, he was young, attractive, and slightly haughty. Everything he said was both alluring and very positive, and I sat simply rapt. After our meeting, certain I'd answered the standard questions flawlessly, I began to relax.

Next came the exhaustive tour of the compound. It was thrilling! I gazed into every open door we passed, taking it all in. The software development lab was the stuff of

Ben's wet dreams, and I couldn't wait to describe its magnificence to him.

A fairly longwinded explanation of the company's infrastructure and fair business practices—*I'd been taught that in business, there was no such thing*—was delivered by a harried and somewhat exhausted-looking woman, quite possibly two years my senior. Though her smile seemed genuine, a trace of desperation lurked in her eyes. We firmly shook hands as she deposited me in a somewhat cramped human resources office.

My stomach growled in the interim, and I wondered where I'd be taken to dinner and in what hotel I'd been booked—not that it mattered. This was a *Big Three*. Surely it would all be swank. I didn't want to jinx my future by jumping to conclusions, but thus far, the day pointed directly towards employment. I stood and smiled wholeheartedly when a sturdy, graying gentleman in a somewhat ill-fitting suit entered the room.

"Good afternoon, Miss Wade. I'm Bernard Barnes." After shaking hands, we settled onto our respective sides of the lacquered oaken desk. He glanced at a sheet of paper, and then with no preamble, said, "We're very interested in tapping into your potential."

I nodded earnestly. "And I'm equally interested in being tapped into—I mean, working for ComSync." His answering smile had me nearly bouncing in my seat.

"We are prepared to offer you a nine-month internship." He presented this as if it were the fabled golden egg.

"I'll take it!" was primed to

explode from my lips, until my mind caught up. "I...um...I didn't apply for an internship," I stammered. "I applied for a fulltime position."

"It is fulltime, I can assure you." Though his lips were still turned upwards, the newfound glint in his eye was slightly unsettling.

I realized this was my time to negotiate. They offer less, I ask for more, both parties meet somewhere in the middle. I'd practiced this in a mock interview session during *Advanced Business Strategies*. My university wanted highly successful alumni primed and ready to heavily contribute to their coffers.

"Well, as far as salary, I really couldn't take less than—"

"There is no salary," he interrupted. "It's an unpaid internship."

I balked. "An *unpaid* internship?"

My vision became spotty, and I realized I had completely stopped breathing.

He glanced over my résumé. "You have no real work experience. Besides, ComSync makes it a practice never to hire individuals directly out of college. It doesn't make financial sense. Of course, you'll learn a great deal about the business, and, after your initial period has expired, if you're one of a select few, you'll have the opportunity to apply for a paid internship."

My mind was awhirl—like the F-5 tornado kind. "By 'unpaid', do you mean that in lieu of salary, I'll receive cost of living provisions and a benefits package?" Surely there was a bright side to this offer. I owned one suit, had about two-hundred dollars in my savings account, and knew absolutely no one in this state—or the ones surrounding it. I was laden with student loans the bank would call in the day I shook hands with the university president and stepped off the stage, and my parents had little money to spare—not that I would ever ask for any. I was self-reliant and far too proud—well, mostly just too proud.

He shook his head no. "I don't mean to sound patronizing, Miss Wade, but we aren't in the business of handouts. If you want to make it in our world, you'll have to be resourceful. Only the most agile will survive our, admittedly, rigorous process. Those are the employees ComSync wants."

This was my first interview, and potentially the best offer I might receive, but it was a slap in the face.

"Mr. Barnes, an internship with your company sounds like an amazing opportunity, and you're absolutely right. I could learn a great deal. I'm as agile as they come—trust me," I added with confidence. "I'd like to think about it for a few days."

His expression became glassy and he chuckled to himself. "We'll need an answer today. ComSync is the top computer company in the world. We have a very long line of applicants who would accept our offer without thinking twice." This was not true—the first part, anyway. They were third in the US and fifth, globally. And while I hadn't heard back from numbers one or two, those flames still burned brightly.

Call me arrogant, call me what you wish, but I was better than this. I hadn't spent the last four years working like the insane to spend my days at ComSync and nights working at Waffle House, sneaking leftover sausages for sustenance and using the pittance of earned cash to pay for a hovel I'd barely see. He hadn't even offered the pale promise of gainful employment.

I looked around the room, thinking of what failure might look like, and then I realized quite suddenly that I was a star just beginning to shine. I was capable and resourceful and intelligent. Further, I respected myself.

"Thank you very much for your time," I said, rising. "I realize an unpaid internship might seem attractive to some, but I'm not convinced it's right for me." I reached across the desk to shake his hand.

He didn't bother standing or even

seeing me to the door. He simply said, "Perhaps you're correct in your assessment, Miss Wade. You clearly lack vision. You may return your visitor's badge to reception on your way out."

My very long drive back to Chicago gave me plenty of time to suffer the sting of his remarks and second guess my decision. My multiple personalities quarreled like siblings over a toy neither truly wanted, but both were loath to part with. I did not suffer from a lack of vision as he suggested. I saw a very bright future ahead of me. What he saw, I decided, was a young and most probably naïve woman. I must be more assertive next time. I prayed there would be a next time. And, petty creature that I was, I promptly vowed to hate ComSync forever.

"How'd the interview go?" Ben asked, literally frothing at the mouth.

"I don't want to talk about it."

"Unacceptable. I want details. What did their headquarters look like—their software development center?" He wore a dreamy expression.

"Here are the two most profound details I'll give: it sucked and I hate them!"

Ben's eyes flared. "It's a *Big Three*. It couldn't have sucked, even if they didn't offer you a position."

"Oh, they offered me a position alright. I turned it down."

"What?!" he shouted. Heads snapped up, eyes glared. "You turned it down? Are you crazy?"

"You know, I don't think I am."

Logging into my station, I planned to construct html code until I forgot all about ComSync. There were a multitude of smaller companies out there—all respectable enough. Though I had no real work experience, as Mr. Barnes so eagerly pointed out, I knew my diploma carried weight. And if the big guys didn't want me, well, others surely might.

3

Cigars and Slobber

Another week passed—one of the longest in my somewhat short life. I trudged to class, sloshing through the thin layer of a late snow. Though a few daffodils breached the crusty blanket, *Spring* breathed promises Northern Illinois would never let her keep.

Ben seated himself beside me, literally humming with energy. I was tired and grumpy from a long week-end of work, and work, and...work. He kept glancing at me, his smile practically neon. I sighed. "Alright, what?"

"I got an interview!" He produced an envelope from his backpack and drew it across his upper lip, sniffing it like a Cuban cigar.

"Where?" I squealed. He needed this so very badly.

"ComTech." He grinned, all toothy.

My chin nearly hit the keyboard. "ComTech," I whispered in awe.

He nodded wildly, his orange wool cap flopping onto my keyboard. "You want me. Tell me you want me."

"I may actually want you," I said with a laugh.

"I'm taking you to dinner. You're celebrating this with me." I really couldn't say no. This was truly epic, and I was so happy for him—happy and obscenely jealous, of course.

As soon as class was dismissed, I raced across to the quad, threw open the post office door, and flung myself against the bank of questionably magical boxes.

"Hey! Watch it, Susan," Brittney spat. Though it was difficult to discern from her typical toxic disposition, she was every bit as on edge as the rest of us. Interviews were nearly as scarce as job offers.

"Oh my god! Oh my god!" she screamed, her hoard of sorority sisters rushing to her side *en masse*. Ben grabbed my arm and hoisted me from the blond melee. "A letter from Com-Sync! Oh my god!" She opened it and began her recitation. "Dear Miss Cox..." Her shrill voice echoed off the tiled walls of the tiny room. I rolled my eyes and smirked; the wording was identical.

Pushing past the erupting pep rally, I jabbed my key into the little lock. "Mail!" I yelped. "Holy Mother of God, I've got mail!" I held up the letter for all to see.

"Give me that," Brittney said, wrenching it from my fingers. Holding it over the surge of bouncing hair, she turned it over several times in feigned curiosity. "Um, it's from a *bank*." She laughed scornfully. "Did you *apply* to a bank, you pathetic creature?"

Snatching the envelope back, I glared at her, and then ran outside. My coat scraped roughly against the crusty wall as I slid down it, chunks of half-melted rock salt gouging painfully into my butt. I slipped open the flap; another overdraft notice.

Could I not even hear from a mid-range company? I thought of city government and hung my head.

"So, um...you wanna come up?" Ben asked, stopping at the entrance to his dorm. It was late, and I'd had two beers. I didn't drink all that often. I was raised a staunch Southern Baptist, and drinking was expressly prohibited—along with about a thousand other things.

I'd successfully transgressed in the "not before marriage" department, but when Tyler pocketed my virginity and walked away a week later, I knew I'd been swiftly and biblically punished. It wasn't long after that that I delivered a similar, swift punishment by walking away from Southern boys, altogether—and Baptists, for that matter. I still tasted bile when I thought of him, the Church...*him*.

The drinks had warmed my stomach and weakened my steadfast resistance. I was also fairly lonely, to be quite honest.

"Um..."

Before I formed an answer, his lips were on mine. The kiss was slightly slobbery and a little off-kilter, and I ended it well before he was ready. If he couldn't kiss properly, I doubted he could do the rest with any skill. Fighting the strong urge to wipe off his spittle, I said, "I've got homework to do. Raincheck?" *Shit! I did not just say that!*

"Raincheck!" he announced triumphantly, breaking out into a

ginormous smile. I cringed as he leaned in for another oral assault, the stench of garlic from the twenty or so bread sticks he'd consumed rushing ahead in white breathy puffs. I successfully dodged it with a quick hug.

"Thanks for dinner. Bye, Ben!"

"Sometimes you dress like a complete hobo," Lexi so kindly informed me the next day.

"What's it to you, Miss *Goodwill?*"

"You've got a guy sniffing around. You ought to at least care about your appearance. You know, make some effort."

"One, I don't want him sniffing around, and two, these sweats are comfortable and very school-spirited."

"Whatever," she cleverly replied, rolling her eyes.

I rolled my eyes back and left for the library in my somewhat hoboish gray sweatpants and blue puffy coat. "At least my hair's not purple!" I snipped to no one in particular.

"And so Mr. Barnes—he told me to call him Bernie. Isn't that so cute?" Her bobble-headed chorus nodded in unison. "Bernie was like, 'Brittney'—I told him to call me that. Adorable, right?" More nodding.

"Dear Lord, just get on with it," I muttered to Ben. Admittedly, this

was far more interesting than programming, but still.

"Brittney, we see real potential in
you," she parroted overdramatically,
her voice ridiculously deep.

"Here comes the best part," I
whispered, nudging Ben.

"ComSync makes it a policy to
never hire individuals directly out of
college—" I slapped my hand on the
table and burst out laughing. She
looked over the heads of her audience
and glowered at me.

"He *said*, 'but for you, we're willing to make an exception'."

"What?!" I was on my feet, locked
in full gape. "They gave you a *job*?! A
paying job?"

"What other kind is there?" She
threw her hands up in the air like I
was a total idiot. "Bernie said I was
the brightest candidate he'd inter-

viewed in years." At my raucous snort, she cocked her head to one side and batted eyelashes that were quite possibly not real. "Have you even *had* any interviews yet?"

"Yes!" I sputtered. "With—" I decided right then that haughtily admitting I'd turned them down would directly lead to additional, more embarrassing questions. All possible scenarios led to her winning. I sank into my seat, muttering mean things. If I thought I'd hated Com-Sync before, I can promise I hated them five times more now.

"Why do you let her get to you like that?" Ben challenged as we crossed the muddy quad to the mail-room. "You got a job with ComSync. You turned it down. Why didn't you just say so?"

"I didn't get a job with them,

okay? I got a stupid unpaid internship. That is *not* a job. She would have called me on it immediately."

"You are, like, the smartest, most capable person I've ever met. I mean, no one should intimidate you."

"She doesn't intimate me."

"Susan, she does. You always let her win. You don't even try standing up for yourself. I don't get it."

"She's just—I—you didn't grow up in a sea of Brittney clones! People like her live to torture people like me. They get the boys, they have the friends—whatever they want."

"And you hand it right to them, don't you?"

"Do you know how many boyfriends I've lost to girls like Brittney? All of them! As soon as I really fall for someone, some Brittneyesque monster smiles real pretty, and I'm flat on my face. One day, my friend, I'm going to meet some woman who can annihilate her type, and I'm going to follow her around like a damn puppy. I'll become her pupil and she'll teach me everything, and then I'll have the power to squash them all."

"Um, Susan, you're scaring me."

I sighed mightily. "Come on, let's just check our boxes."

"Actually, I've gotta go see Professor Garret. Are you working tonight?"

"Why do you even ask such silly questions?"

He smiled crookedly. "See ya then."

There was no one near the counter—no audience, no need for her to contrive the illusion of brow-beaten slave. She knew I wasn't giving her a tip. She gifted me her patented disparaging look as I fired off my latest caffeine-packed ammunition. Petulantly, she snagged a cup from the top of the stack and muttered, "Idiot."

"Why are you working, anyway? You're a spoiled, pampered bi—unpleasant person." She ignored me, nonfat milk sputtering in great gushes. "Why?" I pushed.

"I'm twenty-two," she announced, dropping my change, coin by coin, on the countertop.

"So?"

"*So*, my parents said I was an adult now and had to get a job. They've stopped paying my sorority dues and everything."

"Not your sorority dues!" I gasped in mock-horror.

"Jerks, right? Do you know how much *Fall Formal* cost alone? The dress, the hair, the professional photos, the hotel room—the shot glasses and t-shirts?" she squeaked. "*Spring Bash* is next week and it's even more expensive. They won't pay a penny. It's horrible!"

"Why don't you just quit your sorority?" That seemed the simplest solution—not that I truly cared.

She was the one to gasp this time. "*Appearances*! You can't just walk away from hard-earned popularity. Don't you get it?" She looked over my outfit and formidable hat hair. "No, clearly you don't," she sneered. Though wilting inside, I continued the illusion of indifference. She made a show of looking behind me at the nonexistent line, and then huffed loudly. Goading her, I didn't budge. Finally, she cupped her hand to her ear. "What's that sound? Oh, it's the library calling you, Susan. Go. Away."

The library was in fact calling me, and I smiled all the way there. Though I admittedly knew little about life, this was the day I realized Brittney Cox knew absolutely nothing at all. When the hand feeding the helpless closes, people like her become sad casualties. Never knowing such a hand, I'd been spared similar indignities, I suppose. And oddly, that put a skip in my step.

4

Potato Shrapnel

It was quite possibly the most beautiful thing I'd ever seen. I pressed the envelope to my chest and wept joyfully—okay, actually, I just made a really high-pitched squeaking sound. Another chance at *The Big Three*! I raced back to my room to study every character. There were three-hundred-thirty-two of them to be exact. More than a tweet, less than an essay, all perfect. And Ben was going to die!

ComTech was like Cornell; not Harvard, but still Ivy League. Second only to INTech in total net worth, it was a Southern-based company. This part troubled me, as did the whole of the South. I was comfortable in the North, away from my flock and the accent we'd once shared. Here, I was me: Susan Wade, woman of mystery, someone to be reckoned with, an equal. With only my present and future surrounding me, I felt light and capable. The thought of plunging back into a sea of good ol' boys, heavily-sugared iced-tea, and the conjunction "y'all", gave me faint chills.

But it was *ComTech*. Surely nothing could be wrong with that!

I shakily dialed the number on the

letterhead. A sweet, Southern voice answered, and after a few *uh huh*s, spoke lovely words. "We'd like you to come down for an interview next week, if possible."

"Oh, it's completely possible!" I said, failing to keep pure elation from my voice. "I mean, thank you. I'd like that very much."

"I'll set ya up for Tuesday, the twelfth. How's that?"

"Perfect!" I replied dizzily.

"Expect a packet of information tomorrow." Now that was more like it; something *expressed*. These people understood business. But then I braced myself for the immediate possibility of defeat.

"One question: am I being considered for an internship or an actual job?"

"Well, I assumed you were lookin' for a job."

"You are absolutely correct in that assumption."

"Okay, then. See ya next week."

Just as I'd begun jumping on my bed, my roommate shuffled through the door and dropped her designer backpack on the floor.

"Lexi, I've got an interview, I've got an interview!"

For a moment, she became perfectly still, placidly watching me wave my letter in the air. Then she simply said, "Freak."

"I know, right?" I agreed, jumping in circles and screaming.

"On the house," I said, sliding the

overflowing platter of slightly over-cooked fries towards Ben.

"Susan, you know the way to my heart," he replied as he squirted ketchup over the entire mound.

"The path wasn't all that hard to find." I impatiently glanced back towards the kitchen. "Oops! Gotta go."

I raced across the restaurant with a tray full of sloppily made burgers, thinking our latest fry cook and I needed to have a serious heart-to-heart. *How exactly hard is it to place lettuce and tomato on a patty? This is not rocket science.*

During a blessed lull, I said, "So, when's your Dallas interview?"

"The elevnph," Ben replied around a mouthful of fries. Ketchup dribbled down the side of his mouth, offering up the very image of a rusty-haired, sun-deprived vampire. I handed him a napkin.

"Oh. Mine's the twelfth," I said in such an offhanded fashion he didn't catch it at first. But when the words registered...

"Whuh?!" Potato fragments exploded like shrapnel, pelting the countertop and my chest. "You got an interview with ComTech?"

"Did you think I wouldn't?"

"Well...?" I threw a straw at him. "I mean, not that fast."

Grabbing a dingy rag, I began wiping yuck off my shirt. "Seriously, you should not talk with your mouth full."

He half-assedly dabbed at the table with a wad of napkins and smiled like he was actually helping. "Hey, let's drive down together!"

"You don't even have a car."

"You drive, I'll pay half the gas. It'll save me a shitload in airfare."

I pretended to think about it for a moment. "Deal."

U

"Open that fucking box!" Lexi shouted when I entered the room.

"Shh! It's three in the morning."

I'd decided to make a game of it, though in all honestly, I was simply being belligerent. I didn't care about what was inside, but it was making her crazy—crazier, actually, since I'd placed it very prominently on top of my small dresser. We'd enjoyed an antagonistic relationship since the day she moved in. As she nourished my personal insecurities, I used well-honed passive aggression to lay waste to her in return. *Plus, why was she home so early?*

I shrugged out of my Michelin Man coat and untied my apron, shaking the last of the potato bits into the trash can. Then I simply and quite calmly said, "No."

Her scream, though muffled by the slamming door, still echoed off the drearily painted walls. Laughing hysterically, I fell into bed.

The drive to Dallas was the longest flipping fifteen hours of my life. I sent up prayers to any god that would listen, hoping my car would make it there and back before croaking.

Ben and I swapped seats every three hours. During the first part of the trip, we'd talked non-stop—dreams, hopes, plans for our futures once we'd made our first million, but after running out of topics, I turned on the radio. We then argued music.

Ben was into country, which was intolerable to me on any level. I'd grown up with a classic rock junkie for a father. It would have been an all-out Coke vs. Pepsi war, had I not shared my latest theory with him. You see, I'd very recently begun listening to classical music, because that's surely what sophisticated business professionals did. And of course, if Ben wished to become a sophisticated business professional, he must also embrace this music genre. He not only embraced it, but my entire ideology as well, and we found a nice public radio station.

As we crept farther south, the grass became progressively greener, proving spring did in fact exist. Infant leaves shone brightly, decorating austere limbs, and I'm certain I saw daffodils blaring yellow in front of the occasional *way-too-close-to-the-highway* home. I cracked my window and sank back into my seat, breathing the mystical air.

Crossing over Interstate 40 was a very odd feeling for me. I-40 ran directly through the middle of my hometown, maybe a thousand miles from here. For a moment, I felt intimately linked to this vital, pulsing Southern artery. Of course, that eerie sensation dissipated when Ben hit what looked to be a wayward chunk of rusted tailpipe.

"A flat tire?!" he squawked, as we limped to the shoulder.

"Yes, dammit!" I fired back, seething.

"How can you even tell?"

"Didn't you feel how the car started riding? Any fool knows what that means!" Huffing, I hopped onto the surprisingly scorching asphalt. Sure enough, my tire looked like an Oreo soaked too long in milk.

"Well, what are we going to do?" Ben asked, scratching his head and searching the fairly barren landscape.

"We're going to change it. *Duh.*"

After removing our personal crap from the trunk, I lifted the faded carpet cover and we gazed at the tiny spare. Ben stared at me, utterly perplexed. "Um, maybe we should call a tow truck."

"Do you have money?"

"A hundred bucks."

"I have fifty left after our last fill-up. That won't pay for a tow and patch." Then it dawned on me. "You can't change a tire, can you?"

"Sure I can," he shot back. "You just need a jack and shit—which we don't have."

I rolled my eyes, pulled out the micro-jack tucked in the compartment's corner, and held it up with a smirk. He examined it, turning the squat metal from side to side as if it was a museum piece. I looked to the heavens and shook my head.

"Ben, this is your lucky day. I'm going to teach you how to change a tire." I snatched the jack from his useless hands and dropped to the ground. "Make yourself useful and hand me the tire before a truck squashes us."

"You're not doing it right," he accused, a few minutes later, as I struggled with a particularly belligerent lug nut.

"How the hell would you know?" I grunted, my side crisping on the blacktop griddle.

"I'm a guy."

"And that means what to me?"

"Cars are, like, guy stuff."

I snorted. "Well, it looks like this poor, helpless *girl* is smoking your ass right now."

Thirty minutes later and quite a bit dustier, we edged back onto the highway, lilting to one side on our tiny spare. "I hope to hell this little thing gets us to Texas!"

With the great misfortune of arriving mid-rush hour, it took an extra forty minutes of weaving through traffic before finding our hotel. Soiled, sweaty, and desiccated from driving the last few hours with the windows down, I wanted nothing more than a long shower.

"It sure looks nice," Ben remarked as we parked near the entrance. I forced optimism into my stiff limbs and totally aching butt as we carted our sparse luggage up the carpeted stairs.

Because ComSync had bitten off a large chunk of ego and spat my early naiveté onto the Jersey Turnpike, I had come, quite honestly, expecting little, but the hotel was almost elegant in its modern simplicity—or at least that's what the woman in front of us floridly remarked to her well-dressed companion. While waiting for our keycards, I nudged Ben and smiled as a sudden rush of wild anticipation swept over me.

"This hotel room is moderately stylish at best," I mocked, my nosed turned up in my best impression of a blueblood sophisticate as we surveyed my well-appointed space.

Ben burst out laughing, and then joined in. "The amenities are acceptable, dear, but nothing like that quaint Monacan inn."

I flung open the curtains, revealing the distant Dallas skyline and the lovely park below. "Oh, Chip, the view is atrocious. Call the concierge immediately!" I threw my arm over my forehead as I'd seen Brittney do so often. "We must leave this place at once!"

Ben jerked the phone off the receiver and grinned mischievously.

"I'll do it," he said with a challenging look.

"Do what?"

"I'll totally call and demand a different room."

"Why?"

"Because it would be hilarious."

"Yeah, until ComTech finds out."

"Why would they care?"

That this corporation was paying for nice rooms in a nice hotel was testament to their attitude towards recruits. I wouldn't dare mar that; this was far too important.

"They'll think we're immature assholes and decide not to hire us, that's why! Put the damn phone down, Ben, or I will seriously kill you."

He rolled his eyes. "You worry about the dumbest things. Let's check out *my* room."

We raced down the lavishly carpeted hallway like unleashed children. Ben's room was the last on the left before the fire-escape stairs.

"Well, you've certainly got the better view," I said, snorting.

He rushed to the window and we gazed at the asphalt rooftops of the various wings of the building. He looked at me and smirked. "I'm totally calling now."

On our own for dinner, we managed to find an inexpensive Mexican place within walking distance. As soon as they were placed on the table, we fell on the basket of tortilla chips like desperate wolves.

"These are the best tacos I've ever eaten!" I marveled.

When Ben fed my enthusiasm with a giant smile, I glimpsed the brilliant bits of cilantro clinging fiercely to his teeth like emerald kelp. I fought the extreme urge to say something. He really had to get his "grown-up" act together, or no one would hire him.

On our way back to the hotel, as we walked by a group of lovely, but darkened shop windows, Ben put his arm around me. The arsenal of romantic missives he continued lobbing like snowballs landed unwelcomed. I didn't want a boyfriend, and even if I had, he wouldn't have made my shortlist. Blond, athletic, and painfully handsome had once been my poison of choice, but now, with eyes fully opened, I would choose something quite different; a polished, impressive and powerful professional. Meeting his eyes, I shook my head and pulled away.

5

The V-card

Dallas sprawled like a giant platter of spaghetti; an endless stretch of buildings and suburbia. Rather than one giant headquarters downtown, ComTech's offices were broken into divisions, strewn like tiny meatballs across the city. I learned this only after dropping Ben off at the wrong site, and then enduring his tirade as I delivered him to the correct one.

"Well?" I demanded, pouncing on him as soon as he knocked.

His starry gaze spoke volumes. "Their programming staff is awesome. I can wear jeans and t-shirts, drink Red Bull all day, and work on the finest equipment known to man. I don't even have to shave!" We did a fifteen minute happy dance, and then split a large pizza.

I banged on his door early the next morning. When I got no answer, I pounded louder. "What?" he said groggily. Dressed in striped boxers, his sprouting chest hair and scruffy morning stubble were his only declarations of manhood.

"Tell me honestly, what do you think of my suit?" I modeled it for him in the hallway.

"I think you're beautiful." His face flushed fiercely as he stammered, "I mean, it looks great—perfect. I mean you look perfect. I mean—" He groaned and ran his hand down his face. "I'm going back to bed." He shut the door firmly, and I pivoted and marched towards the elevators.

"Susan, wait!" Ben hustled down the hall, still zipping his jeans. He gripped my shoulders firmly and said, "Kick ass today!" He then gave me a meaningful *go get'em, tiger* look and pecked my cheek.

This interview was not altogether unlike my previous one: the *tell us about yourself* and *why you want to worship us* meeting, the *glorious history of our company* speech, and finally the *our corporate philosophy makes us the*

best in the business tour. It was exhausting and fabulous. I totally busted on my answers, was stunned by the general atmosphere, and saw nothing but smiling faces all day.

A gentleman named Kevin Clarisey took me to dinner. With tawny hair and guileless blue eyes, he was attractive in a thirtyish kind of way.

"It's dangerous to take someone to a genuine Texas barbecue restaurant on an interview, but the ribs are great, and I'll bet you like livin' on the dangerous side. Am I right?"

I stifled a snort, but nodded vigorously. Honestly, I was up for basically anything "ComTech" right now.

"Two beers, darlin'," he said to the waitress as she walked by. His eyes followed her swinging hips until she disappeared. Then he glanced at me. "Ya do drink beer, right?"

"Sure," I replied, all smiles. He wasn't Southern, I noted, but was trying awfully hard to be. Of course, I was trying awfully hard to be a Northern business goddess, so we were even on that score.

As he spoke, Kevin's eyes roamed over me several times, and I began to feel somewhat uncomfortable. I sat up straighter, tried to look super professional, and sent messages in Morse code that though I totally wanted a job with ComTech, I would not sleep with anybody to get it.

"Look, here's the deal," he finally said, dropping his crumpled napkin on his plate. "We need closers—*women* closers. With pretty receptionists, guys have it easy. But with certain business types, a lady's sweet voice can work wonders. We don't have nearly enough females on the sales force." He smiled confidently, but his eyes fell slightly south of mine. "I think you'd make a nice addition. Now be straight up with me," he said soberly. "How comfortable are you with flirting?"

After my coughing fit subsided, I said, "Flirting?"

"The ice-breaker kind. You have to put in two-hundred percent to get through the door and another two-hundred to convince your customer that you have all his answers. You've got to be able to win him over."

I considered the general attitude men held towards women here, and said, "But...it's the South."

"Oh." He let out a generous laugh. "As you well know, Southerners are pretty tightknit. But that set of legs," he said, his eyes trailing knee to ankle, "and your accent will get you through any door down here." Though increasingly disquieted by this particular ribbon of conversation, I tried to look enthusiastic. "Plus, you can clearly dress the part," he added, glancing at my suit.

"Now, I'm not saying clients in the Northeast, or even the West Coast wouldn't fall all over you—I mean, men do love Southern accents," he continued, with a leering smile, "you'd just have to work a lot harder to make them take you seriously." He leaned across the table and lowered his voice. "In sales, you have to work with what you've got. And you've got 'cute and Southern' nailed. Use it!"

I wanted to dump my beer right in his lap. I'd worked like a dog to lose my accent, trying to blend in, to become generic—in speech, anyway. The very last image I wanted to project was "cute and Southern". It was infuriating to learn I'd failed. At this point, only a good cry—oh, and a damned job offer, could quell my internal rage. Focusing exclusively on the latter, I slapped on what I believed was a conspiratorial smile.

A sales position was sounding less appealing by the moment, so I shored my courage and sought another angle. "I'm earning a degree in business, of course, but also in computer technology. What does that side of the company look like?"

"It looks great, but in all fairness, a female computer service rep probably wouldn't go over well in the South. Tools and all," he said, winking.

"But in other parts of the country—"

"Susan, you'll make a fantastic saleswoman, and I can promise you'll have a great time working for ComTech. We're a solid company with lots of room for career growth." Then he placed his hand lightly on my arm. "Now how about another beer?"

Ben threw open his door before I even knocked. "How did it go? Did they love you?"

I sighed and flopped on his bed. "Yeah, they loved me, alright. I'll be very surprised if I don't get an offer—or a marriage proposal," I muttered.

"That's awesome!" He flopped down beside me and cradled his head in his hands, mirroring me, our elbows touching. "This is my dream job," he finally said, rolling on his side. "If ComTech doesn't make me an offer, I will seriously jump off the Hancock Building."

"They'll make you an offer." I smiled genuinely. "They will."

"I was thinking...if we both get hired, we can be, like, roommates. It would save us money, plus we don't know anybody down here. What do you think?" His eyes were bright and dreamy.

"That's not a bad idea. I'll need as much cash as possible. My dress code's going to be a bit different than yours. I'll also need a car that's a little less redneck." My car was prehistoric, bright orange, and looked like a NASCAR reject.

"I love your car! It's, like, retro."

"I'll sell it to you—cheap."

He smiled widely.

"Hell, if I get a decent offer, I'll give you the damn thing."

"Deal."

There was no magic in the air, no hearts racing—at least not mine, but he leaned over and kissed me. His tongue flailed around my mouth like an air-deprived fish, but loosened up by alcohol and filled with excitement and utter gratitude that I'd successfully survived the grueling day, I tolerated it. And when his hand began edging towards my breast, I didn't stop him.

Though losing the oral battle, I was getting a little turned on, and I welcomed the sensation when he finally reached his goal—which took about ten minutes. It hadn't taken *that* long to lose my damn virginity.

He rather ineptly squeezed through the blouse's material, seemingly incapable of kissing and fondling at the same time.

Becoming increasingly annoyed, I shifted a little to try to help him, but to no avail. Seducing a woman that was potentially open to it just wasn't that hard. When he left my breast and set out on his sluggish descent, I realized it was going to take him the better part of an hour to reach my hem. In utter frustration, I broke the kiss and sat up, but after taking in his flushed face, dilated pupils, and his expression of determined hope, I suddenly understood what I hadn't bothered to consider: Ben was a virgin.

Perhaps, for some, there is a certain fulfillment of ego that comes with taking someone's virginity.

Based on my own experience, how-
ever, I felt differently. Receiving such
a gift, such a precious thing, was a
great honor. Mine had been a mere
gumball machine prize to its recipi-
ent—something to be played with
briefly and then tossed aside once
another quarter was placed in the
slot. I still felt the ache and anger of
my misplaced trust, my impotent
love.

Of course, the next few partici-
pants hadn't mattered all that much;
they'd gotten their thrill, and I, the
resentment of quick dismissal and
latent regret. With sour memories, I
faithfully watered the saplings of
hatred that had sprouted from my
choices—*and theirs*, and with every
inch they grew, I added another layer
to the wall surrounding that suckling
forest.

Because I did not share his feelings, did not feel love for him, did not even desperately desire him, I was not deserving of Ben's treasure. Someone better than me should have it—someone capable of loving him in return, of possibly even exchanging gifts in mutual discovery.

I truly wanted that for him, so I boldfaced lied. "I'm sorry, Ben, but you're moving too fast. I'm really not ready for this. Plus, I'm super tired, and we've got a long drive tomorrow." His answering look was that of a dog caught chewing an expensive dress shoe.

He scrambled to his knees and held up his hands. "Susan, I'm sorry, I'm sorry. It's just, I really like you...and I think, you know, maybe you like me, too."

I smiled at his delusional assessment.

"Come back." He patted the bed. "I'll take it way slower. We won't do anything you're uncomfortable with."

I bit my cheek to keep from smiling and shook my head no. "You're just more man than I'm ready for." I leaned over and kissed his cheek. "Goodnight, Ben."

6

Pandora's Box

The job offer was perfection—well, sort of. Close. Definitely close! It was in the sales division—commissioned sales; small salary, high potential. I stared at the letter for a long time. ComTech had treated me well, put me up in a nice hotel for two nights, taken me to dinner, given me a per diem which paid for my tire patch, and according to the premium stock paper in my hand, granted me generous time to make a decision. Overall, I liked them. Kevin was right; I could do well there. I could be happy. Yes, I could will myself to be happy.

"Mom, I got a job."

"Glory be!" she sang into the phone. When I didn't join in with some sort of amen, she said, "Honey, you don't sound too happy about it."

"I'm extremely happy. It's with a Texas firm."

"My prayers have been answered! You're comin' home."

"Texas isn't 'home'," I quipped.

"Well, you know what I mean. It's the South." Then she whispered, "Did you get the package?"

I'd altogether forgotten about it, and a pang of remorse barreled through me. "I—"

"Oh," she murmured, her spirited

voice retreating into its dank cave. "Your daddy wants to talk to you."

"Give me that phone!" he growled. "Susie, how are ya, princess?"

"I got a job."

"Took long enough. Ya can't stay in school forever."

"Daddy, I've been here the normal amount of time."

After a moment of silence, his question thoroughly shocked me. "You still need us to come up for graduation?"

Hurt colored my answer. "I, I don't *need* you to come...I guess." *But you ought to, dammit!* "All the other parents are, though."

"It's an awful long drive from here." I heard my mother's stifled whimper, and my own chin began trembling. Drawing breath had suddenly become difficult.

"I'm talkin' on the phone here, Polly. Take your snivelin' someplace else! Susie, your mamma's such a—"

"I've gotta go. Bye, Daddy."

I sank onto the edge of Lexi's bed and dropped my face in my hands, pledging then and there that I would never marry, never suffer such indignities. Once I'd calmed myself, I lifted the box from my dresser. A Hallmark foil seal was affixed to the envelope's flap. I tore through it and fished out the card. The words were sappy, religious, and irrelevant. The note that fell out was diamond encrusted.

Dear Susie,

I love you like the sun, the moon, and the stars. You are doing what I always dreamed of, and I want you to get the best job you can and become an amazing woman. Always remember, you can have anything you want in life if you set your mind to it. What's in the box is from me. PLEASE don't tell your daddy what I got you. I've been saving my money for a long time, hoping you'd graduate and need this. I surely hope you like it.

I'm so proud of you. I can't wait to watch you walk across that stage. It'll be the happiest day of my life.

Love you always,

Mom

I dashed the tears with my sleeve. She hadn't been afforded the opportunity that I, now on the cusp of graduation, enjoyed. The bright future she'd planned had been denied her. I'd seen to that in my abject innocence. I would burn Mom's words across my heart. I would make them my very mantra. I opened the stout box.

Too much tissue covered what was a true thing of beauty. I lovingly ran my fingers across the supple leather, and then twisted the shiny brass latch in a full state of awe. The briefcase had slits for company pens and the stunning business cards I would soon possess. I quickly swiped away the salty droplet that landed on the strap, and then holstered it over my shoulder. It was weighted perfectly—or would be when it contained all the necessary paraphernalia.

Undoubtedly expensive and well beyond my mother's meager means, she must have skimped on all things self for a very long time to afford it. It infuriated me that she had to do this; to sneak around and hide things.

I breathed in the pale, fresh leather scent, and after carefully returning it to the colorful box, displayed it on Lexi's pillow. I then pulled out my laptop, hit voice recorder, and began reading from my *Modern Business Theory* textbook in the most non-Southern accent I could possibly muster.

Ben hummed with excitement the next morning. "I just accepted ComTech's offer."

"That's so flipping awesome, Ben!"

We'd danced like demons the moment we read our letters, and then celebrated with baskets of fries, milkshakes, and leftover hamburgers last night. Having now accepted his dream job, he would no longer entertain thoughts of suicide. Me? I still had a stray few.

"We are now ComTech professionals." He fist-pumped the air.

"People should, like, have to pay to touch us!"

That night, I fell into bed later than usual. A band of staggering fools had burst through the doorway just before closing, demanding service. Though physically exhausted, my mind kept sleep at bay. Unlike Ben, I hadn't accepted ComTech's offer, yet. My head and heart were locked in a heated battle, each side fully committed to its cause, and I feared all the wrong reasons were winning out.

This was a tremendous opportunity, and I could always request a transfer later. Putting my computer expertise aside, I could prostitute myself to sell their products. I could do that. I absolutely could do that...*couldn't I?* Sleep won out maybe five minutes before my alarm sounded.

"You look awful," Ben remarked when I withered into my chair.

"I haven't accepted the job, yet, and I don't know why."

"What?! That's a no-brainer, Susan. It's ComTech for God's sake. Call them right after class. Do it before they change their minds."

"After class," I mumbled.

7

Nazi Tweezers

I let an entire week slip by. This decision was by far the most pivotal of my life, but something—an almost tangible entity—was preventing me from picking up the phone. The job didn't feel right, and I was terrified of making the wrong choice. But there was no other choice—none that I would consider, anyway, and certainly not with ComTech's arms open wide. I needed to move forward, but it was a little like trying to muster feelings for Ben. Though he was a great guy, who'd probably give me the world if I asked, I just couldn't make myself commit.

Lost in paralysis, I meandered into the post office, fully expecting the usual nothingness. Other than continuing the ritual, I don't know what I hoped to find there. I'd already received the gift of a lifetime, but I wandered in daily just the same, wishing, I suppose, for something I dared not dream of.

I flipped open my *porthole of the unloved* and peeked inside. Something blinked back; something sleek and tan and very professional-looking. With shaky hands, I coaxed the sturdy envelope from the darkness, careful not to further bend it.

The return address caused my entire respiratory system to shut down.

I skidded around the corner and slammed right into Ben's chest. Though he was the one I should have shared this with—even asked him to open it for me, instead I just yelled, "Move!" and kept running.

The commons was approximately the size of a football field, and I ate up the frozen turf like a running back, not even slowing as I burst into the dorm. Several girls flung obscenities at my back as I flew by, their books and papers scattering in my wake.

"It's miraculous!" I panted to a rather surprised Lexi. "I got a letter!"

"Yeah, I remember the first time I ever got mail—"

"Lexi, it's from INTech!"

My chest heaving, I carefully slid open the flap, praying all the while that it was an interview invitation. The embossed seal on the water-marked letterhead literally gleamed, and I took a moment to absorb this potentially perfect moment. I wanted to work for INTech so badly I would joyfully scrub their floors with my toothbrush, but fear had almost kept me from applying; fear of utter rejection, of them sneering at my unworthiness. And though I thought pretty highly of myself in general, there was reality: a cute Southern girl in pretty pink suit.

Taking shallow sips of air, my fingers trembled as I read down the page.

"You want a paper bag or something?" Lexi asked sardonically. "You look like you're gonna pass out."

"Shh!" I whispered, waving her off. "Dear Miss Wade..." Her pixie face blurred as my eyes misted. "Holy crap, I have an interview!"

"You've had two interviews. You're, like, super business girl or some shit."

"But this...this is *INTech*," I whispered reverently.

"So?"

"*So*, they're the greatest computer company in the world. They are actually number one! They're the Harvard of computer companies!" I pulled up their website to show her, and suddenly realized that those beautiful, powerful, smart-looking women on the screen were all dressed in...black. I gasped.

"Lexi, I can't wear my suit!"

"Duh. I told you it was ugly. Take the train into Chicago and buy a real one."

"I don't have any money," I said,

fully panicked. "I spent it all on gas getting to flipping Dallas and back. I can't afford real clothes—not like these people are wearing."

She rolled her eyes as if—well, I don't know why, actually. "Looks like funeral crap to me."

I turned on her. "You, with your purple hair, and your freaky clothes, and, and your poor taste in jewelry," I shouted, glaring at her tarantula necklace. "You wouldn't know a business suit if it bit you on the ass!" Then I pointed to the lovely leather backpack she insisted on dragging across the ground like a bag of garbage. "You know nothing about nice things. In fact, you know nothing about fashion at all!"

She looked quite literally shocked, and for a brief moment remained speechless. Then she exploded. "I know everything about fashion. *Everything*! I just don't give a shit about it!" She roughly pushed past me, slamming her backpack against the wall on her way out.

"But why are you even considering INTech?" Ben's demeanor had slowly transformed from insolent outrage to deflated sulkiness in the hour since I'd delivered the earth-shattering news. The counter before him had already been wiped clean of his spent food fragments, and he now absently nursed the chocolate milkshake I'd made to comfort him.

"Because, it's the best frigging company in the world!" I repeated for the seventh time. "I've dreamt of working for them since forever. I monitor their stock prices. I did a whole project on them in *business ethics*!"

"But you already have a job."

"Offer, Ben. I have a job *offer*. I haven't accepted yet." I hadn't exactly shared that part with him, mostly because I was running out of rags.

"You haven't?!" he sputtered. "Are you crazy?" He gaped so marked that I could count his molar fillings—three, to be exact. "Why risk losing a real job for a dream?"

"It's not a dream!" I screeched. "It's real! I have a letter. It's real."

"The invitation is real, the job offer doesn't exist. And it probably won't."

"It might, you ass. No one else has even gotten an interview with them!"

"My point," he said flatly, crossing

his arms. "ComTech not only inter-viewed you, they want to hire you. *H.I.R.E.* Give you *money*. Nobody else has done that."

He was right and it hurt. Sure, I was slipping through the giant's front door for a day, but in all fairness, it was only a day. And at the end of it, I might get booted right back down the beanstalk. *Oh, but the view...*

"You're jealous. That's what you are. You wish you had this chance."

"I don't need this chance. I have a job. A *real* job. Right now, you've got nothing."

"Restaurant's closed. Go home." I pointed to the door.

"Seriously, Susan, don't screw this up. We belong in Texas—the two of us." His longing look touched a nerve.

"You only care about my future if

you're in it. Philadelphia is where I belong, not Texas. I don't want to live in the South—ever. Don't you get it? I *hate* the South!"

"That's a stupid reason. The South is great. It's warm, like, all the time, and everybody I met there was super friendly and helpful. What's not to love?"

"You have no idea what you're talking about. You're from frigging Michigan. Those people down there may have seemed charming, but inside, they were cursing you. You're an outsider, you'll never fit in there, and you won't even understand why. Let me explain it to you in their terms: you're a Damn Yankee, and that will never change!"

His arms dropped to his sides, and he groped for words that clearly weren't coming. I couldn't begin to help him understand the finer nuances of the society into which he was happily loping. Through a plethora of sweet words and glowing smiles, he would be patronized, constantly scrutinized, and unquestionably cast aside. It was hard enough surviving there holding a blood ticket. He had no chance.

It was during this stretch of heated silence that my own hesitation about ComTech became crystalline. It wasn't the position, the salary, or even the semi-prostitution that bothered me. I simply couldn't live in the South again. I couldn't do it, no matter what was at stake.

"You're messed up!" he finally retorted.

"Soon, you'll be, too! Now leave."

Mopping wasn't drudgery tonight. I had INTech to dream

about, and Ben's words to fuel my strength.

U

I awoke the next morning with Lexi straddling me, an implement of torture pointed at my forehead.

"What the hell?!"

"Don't move or you'll screw this up."

"Again, I will ask, *what the hell?*"

In horror I watched Lexi's hand approach, the tweezers menacing, her expression that of a surgeon.

"Lexi?"

"I said, don't move! Your eyebrows are like bushes. People in Philly don't have bushy eyebrows."

"There's nothing—ouch! Stop it!" I winced, and my nose began to run.

"Beauty comes with sacrifice," she sneered.

"What do *you* know about it?" I gasped.

"Shitloads! Do you know who my freak of a mother is? Huh? Do you?" Lexi's breath reeked of cigarettes and anger, and I dared not even flinch. "She's a fucking beauty Nazi. She's the Hitler of beauty!"

Through my haze of stinging pain, Lexi's words expanded into images I'd never imagined. From this unusual vantage, I studied her face analytically. It was perfectly shaped, I realized: petite features, large, lovely cobalt eyes, high cheekbones. There was beauty hidden beneath her outrageous hair and ghoulish makeup. Great beauty.

"Growing up was a nightmare!" she growled, taking her life's frustrations out on my forehead. Two years with her emotional door padlocked, and I suddenly saw light through the keyhole.

"Why?"

"Shut up or I'll make you bleed," she hissed, wickedly plucking one innocent hair at a time, conjuring images of Vietnamese war camps. Her voice became reedy. "I couldn't eat anything but nuts and rice cakes. I was constantly waxed and plucked and made-up. I had to wear the most ludicrous outfits."

"I don't understand."

"I was a model. She made a fucking Barbie doll out of me. She said the only way to success was through beauty. That's how she'd made it. Fucking bitch." She looked at me through solemn eyes. "It's not, you know."

"I know, Lexi. It's not." I couldn't believe we were having this conversation. I wore my painful childhood scars like a badge, but hers? Hers were spray painted across a giant billboard—one I'd never taken the time to read.

With a last gouging yank that left me breathless, she said, "You're done. You look halfway decent." She then put her nose to mine, her eyes hard as cut sapphires. "Never lose this arch again. *Ever!*" She hurled the tweezers at her closet door like a poison dart and rolled off me. "Now do your damn nails—neutrals only! And if you ever wear pink again, so help me God, I'll cut you!"

Since the day she'd dumped her mountain of clothing on the closet floor and claimed the bed by the window, I'd always assumed her mother was a wealthy, bored housewife with an untreatable shopping addiction. But the mention of her success left me wondering.

"What does your mother do for a living?"

"Shut up, Susan!" She stormed to her desk and holstered her backpack.

"Lexi? Answer my question! What does she do?"

She stopped with her hand on the doorknob and stood there for a moment, shoulders hunched inward as if she was injured. Finally, she turned to me with the most excruciatingly defeated expression. "She's Fashion Editor for *Vogue* Magazine." Her voice then became barely audible. "Are you happy, now? Are you totally, fucking happy?" She wiped the streaks of drooling mascara with her sleeve and fled the room, taking all of the air with her.

8

Ninja Attack

The night before I flew out—*sounds so cool, right?*—I yanked open the heavy dorm door and skipped down the hall. Ticking off my mental list, I realized I'd forgotten toothpaste. I stalked to my toiletries bin and stuffed a tube in my already bulging bag. Though I was only staying one night, I didn't want to take any chances.

After shedding my grease-stained

clothes, I glanced around my general space in search of some semi-clean pajamas. The gasp barely escaped my lips before I turned statue.

Lying on my bed was the most delicious black business suit I had ever seen. So finely tailored, in fact, I couldn't begin to estimate its cost. A crisp, white, million-thread-count cotton blouse with actual French cuffs winked from inside the jacket. On the floor below were sharp-toed, six-inch heeled, patent leather pumps that could easily serve as weapons in a ninja attack. Like Sleeping Beauty drawn to the fabled spinning wheel, I couldn't stop myself from picking them up. My reflection shone brightly in their dazzling sheen.

I snatched up the note on my pillow. Written on elegant, monogrammed stationary I'd never seen before, was the following:

Susan,

You're weird, you talk funny, and you can't dress worth shit. Wear this to your interview so you don't embarrass yourself.

Lexi

PS. I hate your fucking ass.

I wiped at the tears trickling down my smiling lips.

Though I waited up until my eyes drooped, Lexi didn't return that night, and I didn't see her before leaving the next morning. Ultimately, this didn't surprise me. She knew I would hug the living crap out of her, and her rampart-like emotional wall would never allow it.

Having filled the briefcase with every scrap of paper INTech had sent, I quadruple checked the boarding passes tucked into the inner pocket. *Business class.* I wasn't sure what that meant, exactly, but it sounded really impressive. And since I was a soon-to-be businesswoman, that's surely where I belonged.

Butterflies fluttered in swarms with every train bounce on the way to the airport. I'd never flown before for two reasons: one, our family had nowhere near the means to afford it, and two, my parents rarely crossed North Carolina's state borders unless there was an all-out emergency, such as *It's the Fourth of July and we don't have any firework!* (Legally sold in South Carolina), or *Lord have mercy, we're out of apple butter!* (Virginia apparently had an endless supply).

Chicago O'Hare was massive, and I felt rather awestruck as I wove through the bustling throngs of men, women, children, and the occasional Seeing Eye dog. Long lines of restless travelers, spilling well past the roped off security area, twisted like irritated snakes. I tried to look aloof and bored, though I buzzed with excitement.

After ten minutes of sheer immobility, I noticed a much shorter line filled with impeccably dressed fliers holding briefcases and talking on their phones. A small placard read *Business Class* just like my ticket. I crept over and stood behind a tall brunette, whose hair was wound in a loose, sophisticated chignon.

As my eyes ran over her, I realized it wasn't just her lovely hair that mesmerized me; this woman embodied professionalism. Her spiked heels reflected the light spilling through the glass ceiling high above, and her suit fit her form as if personally made for her. The smoky-blue blouse she wore was so lovely I wanted to touch it. Hers was the very look I must aim for.

Glimpsing my own disproportionate reflection in a chrome-wrapped column, I realized with a shock that Lexi had put together an ensemble not altogether dissimilar. I would find some way to thank that purple-haired girl, if it was the last thing I ever did.

Most probably sensing my probing eyes, the woman glanced at me. I smiled sheepishly. She lifted a perfectly arched eyebrow, and without a degree of warmth, pulled out her phone and put her back between us.

It wasn't long before I was standing before security's conveyor belt. After setting my beautiful briefcase and well-worn bag onto the metal rollers, I surveyed the quality luggage riding ahead of mine, fervently wishing I could afford one of those sleek carry-ons displayed in the large shop windows.

"Shoes?" the guard with the shiny gold badge and world-weary expression said.

"Huh?"

"Shoes." I dumbly looked at him and he rolled his eyes. "You have to put your shoes in a bin."

I glanced anxiously at the veritable tower of containers well out of reach, and then at the sizeable swell of fidgety people behind me stuffing their paraphernalia *and shoes* into gray plastic trays. A well-dressed savior snorted as he shoved a tub in front of me.

"Thanks," I muttered.

I quickly slipped off my incredibly uncomfortable footwear and passed through an odd and intimidating chamber. No alarms sounded, and the officer holding a hand wand looked past me. I stepped to the other side of the x-ray machine, wondering vaguely if it would give me cancer, and collected my things as they slid past. Propping myself against the conveyor belt to wrestle my shoes back on, the man behind me huffed impatiently, and I suddenly felt like a complete poser. *One day, my friend, you'll meet a different Susan Wade.*

Long, sleek escalators descended into something akin to the mouth of Hell, and I was deposited into a massive throat, choked with travelers.

Lost and jostled, I wandered down the long, congested hallway. To my right, an encased train halted with a loud hiss. A hollow and echoing voice sharply droned, "The train is leaving the station, please step away from the doors." As it sped into oblivion, I took my place in line, hoping I was in the right place.

"Excuse me," I finally asked a confident-looking, uniformed flight attendant. "Is this the way to concourse C?"

"No, *E*," she replied.

"Oh. I'm trying to get to Philadelphia."

"The flight board is down the hall. You can find departure and arrival gates and times there." Taking in my panicked expression, she smiled faintly. "You'll figure it out."

I did find the board with a bit

more assistance and studied it like the Bible. My plane was on time, though it had been moved to—*wait, now I'm supposed to go to* E? I growled softly and marched back to the train. When it hurtled to a stop, passengers burst forth in an explosion of suits and bags. Before they were fully out of the way, the desperate travelers before me poured into the small space, shimmying around the bolus. There was a sudden bark of the recorded message, and the doors shut right in front of me. I was becoming frantic.

Turning away, I began trekking on foot. Though afraid I'd look the complete fool, I wanted to run full-out. Blessedly, after speed walking for what seemed a mile, I came to what could only be described as an urban legend: a moving sidewalk. In every way, it resembled a flattened escalator. Stepping onto it, I promptly lost my balance and nearly fell on my ass. Once firmly righted, I kept an iron grip on the rubber railing and stood stock-still as the world rapidly passed by. *Now* this *is the way to travel!*

"Coming through," a man yelled over his shoulder as he hustled past. In quick succession, another followed, rudely jostling me.

"Hey!" I yelled.

As the carpet raced towards me, a recording barked, "Warning, the moving sidewalk is ending." *Duh.*

Turns out, when a fast moving object—say, a moving sidewalk—intersects with an immobile object—a floor, for argument's sake—energy is transferred. Also gravity is involved. These are laws of physics. Since I, like so many, am ruled by said laws, in this particular example, the energy transferred was in the form of my body, and the gravity part sent it crashing to the floor—sprawled, I might add.

Scrambling, as the passengers behind me yelped and tried not to step on me, I grabbed my spilled papers and briefcase, and hobbled to the sanctuary of the nearest ladies room. I scurried into the first stall and sank, fully clothed, onto the commode seat. Though my skinned knee wasn't bleeding much, the hose were trashed. I shimmied out of them, cursing under my breath, and stuffed them in the sanitary napkin container.

The floor length mirror mocked me. My hair was disheveled, my blouse, a bunched and wrinkled mess, and my mascara was threatening to run. I straightened and tidied, and then blotted my eyes with a scratchy paper towel. After several deep breaths and the internal pep talk of a lifetime, I removed a clip from my now scuffed briefcase and twisted up my hair in vain imitation of that sophisticated woman's coif I'd seen earlier. *She* could have handled this. *No, she never would have fallen in the first place!*

9

Flying the Friendly Skies

I only needed to pass by four rows before I found my seat. The plane was massive, and I fought the strong urge to walk its length just to see what an actual fuselage looked like. Down the duel pathways, people clogged the aisles, stuffing large purses, carry-on bags and small suitcases into the overhead compartments. The flight attendants walked by after most were settled and began closing the lids with loud smacks. I leaned back, preparing for the unknown.

A uniformed woman spoke informatively about exits, flotation devices, and loss of oxygen. I listened, rapt. The man beside me completely ignored her.

"Sir, you must turn off your electronic device now."

"Okay. Sure," he said brightly. But as soon as she passed, he rolled his eyes and continued texting. When she returned and repeated herself more sternly, he pocketed it and glanced at me with a sly smile.

Somewhat flustered, I said, "Hi, I'm Susie—Susan, I mean."

"Scott."

"Where are you from?"

He looked at me oddly. "You mean what company?"

"No, I mean where did you

grow—I mean, yes." I felt a strong blush creeping up my cheeks.

An absolutely standard North Carolina question, where you grew up said certain things about you—an identity to which one could relate, and perhaps extend conversation through discovered similarities. *Oh, and piously judge you.* Of course, the flipside of that useful coin was that my Southern roots would be unearthed, and my cool, business persona shattered. Kevin Clarisey's painful words echoed in my head. I must be taken seriously. I met Scott's eyes with a perky smile.

"General Electric," he answered casually.

I struggled for something intelligent to say in return. "I hear their stock's doing well."

He looked at me like I had three heads. "Not at the moment."

"Oh." A full minute of silence lapsed as the flight attendants scurried around, preparing for takeoff. I couldn't admit to this man that this was my first flight, and that everything was just wondrous and a little scary, so I said, "I'm going to Philadelphia for a job interview."

"That's nice," he replied absently, fishing an airline magazine from the seat pocket.

"With INTech," I continued. "You know, the greatest computer company in the world?" Someone snorted in the row behind me, and Scott raised his eyebrows and smirked.

"Well, I hope you're tougher than you look."

"Why?" I asked, totally affronted.

"Don't you know about INTech?"

"Yes—no, I mean, what do you mean?"

An unsettlingly wicked smile formed on his lips, and he leaned towards me. "Rumor has it, INTech *eats* their young."

I narrowed my eyes. "I'm totally tough, and, and INTech is a great company!"

He made a noncommittal *hmm*ing sound, and then proceeded to ignore me, becoming engrossed in the flipping of pages. Unable to further connect, I gave up and stared out the window.

Anxiety, excitement, and abject fear swirled inside me as the plane jolted suddenly and then began slowly moving backwards. It then maneuvered into a line behind a small army of aircraft. The captain introduced himself over the crackling loudspeaker, and said we were eighteenth in line for takeoff. A collective groan flooded the cabin, and for the next twenty minutes or so, the plane jerked forward and then stopped, the engines ramping each time, only to quiet again. I'd lost track of the snail-like movement as the engines thrust yet again. But this time, rather than the recurrent aborted whine, the whistle became an urgent scream.

Rising from the earth is a feeling I'll surely never forget. Pulled into my seat and weightless at the same time, I grinned stupidly and pressed my nose to the Plexiglas window, watching the runway, the airport, and Lake Michigan fall away. The fluffy clouds above made large shadows on the far-away ground, and I was mesmerized.

Everything was smooth and

peacefully thrilling, until the plane banked hard to the right and I felt a falling, completely out of control sensation. Certain we were crashing, my eyes shot to Scott, who looked completely bored. I death-gripped the armrests until we leveled out and breached the snowy barrier that became carpet to an endless blue dome. Suddenly, the plane seemed to slow, and the engines assumed a steady drone. I breathed a well-earned sigh of relief, unsure whether the terror was worth the thrill.

The flight was quite calm after that as far as I could tell. As soon as the illumined *fasten seatbelt* sign went off, Scott pulled out his phone and mercilessly played a video game without muting the volume in the slightest. It would have been annoying had it not been an excellent distraction.

As there was really nothing to do over the next two hours, I flipped through all the magazines in the pouch at my knee, and then pulled out my briefcase and shuffled through INTech's paperwork, focusing on the unknowns that lay ahead. Regardless of how it played out, tomorrow would surely be the most important day of my entire life—my personal Olympics.

A chime sounded and the captain mumbled something over the intercom that I didn't quite catch. We were instructed by the attendant to fasten our seatbelts and prepare for final descent. I won't lie; I got a little freaked, fearing this experience would be as terrifying as takeoff. But when we escaped the turbulent cloudbank, an entirely new world lay below: skyscrapers of an unfamiliar city, tiny ant cars and busses moving in steady streams, the Atlantic Ocean in the distance, and I altogether forgot I was even flying.

Landing was far less interesting than takeoff. The city gently floated towards us until I felt I could reach out my hand and touch it. A jolting bump was followed by a groaning scream. My body was thrust toward the seat in front of me and then back, as we slowed to a gentle roll. *Easy-peasy.*

As soon as the beast docked, seat-belts clicked like rapid fire photography, and bags were yanked from their compartments. Passengers filled the aisles like racehorses, only to then stand and awkwardly look at one another for what seemed ten minutes. I felt kind of stupid, to tell the truth—that is, until the door finally flung open and we hustled out in a well-ordered stampede. It was far less glitzy than I'd imagined.

I bled into the swiftly flowing human river, feeling more confident. I had survived my first flight. I avoided the moving sidewalk entirely, and based on that awful experience, the train as well. Instead, I simply walked, admiring the beautiful mosaics, the framed posters of our most historic monuments, and the Liberty Bell replica in the Plexiglas case. Philadelphia.

10

Glamorous

A line of yellow taxis stretched down the curb like children waiting for Santa. So many people were waving that several cabs almost collided, swooping in to claim their willing prey. I'd hailed a cab in Chicago a couple of times, so I added my raised hand to the mix.

"Hey! That's mine!" I yelled as a man dove into the taxi I'd finally flagged. Shrugging, he offered me a look that was one part *my mistake* and two parts *tough shit*. This act was consistently repeated until I finally threw an elbow and launched myself into a smelly backseat.

"Where to?" the man asked amiably. Of course, it took three tries before I correctly deciphered the words through the accent he wielded. *Russian, maybe?*

Negotiating the historical district, I listened intently as the driver doled out all kinds of obscure facts not covered in my high school social studies class. What I only belatedly realized was he had taken the most convoluted route possible, and my fare was astronomical. I gave him my meanest look and tipped him scantily, hoping all the while I'd have enough money left for train fare back to Evanston.

Before stepping under the hotel's

crimson awning, I took a moment to survey my surroundings. It wasn't that the city was overwhelming, or the buildings especially high, it was sheer anticipation that sent shivers through me—the thrill that this metropolis might one day become my own. All I need do was convince the world's most powerful computer company that I was INTech material, that I was the next great thing.

Though my hotel room was far nicer than any I'd ever seen, and my bed was huge and overstuffed and unbelievably comfortable, sleep came in fitful bouts. I awoke before my alarm went off and cancelled my *just in case* wake-up call. I took my time showering, preparing my answers, churning through every possible scenario. As I meticulously straightened my hair, I again rehearsed the questions I'd ask in return—to let them know I was interviewing them as well.

Dressed in my once again crisp and magnificent suit, I shoved a muffin down my throat, gulped too hot coffee, and spilled into the street, the sidewalk's press immediately consuming me. Jammed at the crosswalk, the crowd surely one-hundred deep, it took two traffic lights before I reached the asphalt.

U

I didn't mean to block the walkway, gawking like a tourist, but INTech's headquarters was simply stunning. The towering crystal structure with its wide and sturdy wings offered the very image of a rocket preparing for launch; a tower of hope amidst a city of towers. My mission: to explore this strange new world, to seek out a new life in this new civilization, to boldly never ever mention I liked *Star Trek*.

Suddenly, I was caught in a current of beautifully dressed professionals flowing into a stunning two-story atrium lined with tropical plants. The symphony of footsteps echoed fortune and power and all things perfect. This was the stuff of dreams, my Mecca.

The bank of elevators stared ahead like the entrance to so many treasure-filled caves. I walked assertively to the security counter, announced myself, signed in, claimed my visitor's badge, and then waited in calm impatience for my escort. I would do anything to get this job, to be part of this. And if they only offered me an unpaid internship, well, I would take it and sleep on a park bench if necessary.

"Miss Wade?"

"Yes!" I replied, standing quickly. The woman held out an extremely confident hand coupled with a new-found and glimmering smile. I tried to hide my shock. She was the elegant woman from the airport—the very one I so hoped to emulate. She had no idea who I was, of course. And why would she? She was a goddess, and I, a mere mortal.

"Welcome to INTech." Her eyes roamed over me as we waited by the lustrous steel doors. "Your shoes are gorgeous!" she suddenly exclaimed.

"Thank you," I said, internally beaming. Then she actually bent over to get a better look.

"Are those Jimmy Choos?" Certain she was trying to put me at ease—*really* trying, I simply smiled. "My God, they are!" She rose to full height and looked down at me with a raised brow. "This style won't be available until August. I've already pre-ordered them. How did you get these?"

Several responses popped into my head. *My roomie gave 'em to me* and *I have no flipping idea what you're talking about* were running neck and neck, but then the Devil took me by the hand and I smiled smugly. "I know someone at *Vogue*." She gasped and stared at me with an expression nearing awe, and I truly thought I might die on the spot.

As the elevator rocketed heavenwards, I inhaled deeply, thinking of firm handshakes and focused eyecontact. And when the doors opened, I stood still, my eyes misting, my heart wishing Ben could see this, know this moment, understand why *this* was my dream.

The great labyrinth was filled with myriad cubicles, sleek desks, and a flurry of serious-minded people missioned with important tasks. Unlike the generally dour aura I'd sensed at ComSync, or the casual, almost buoyant feel of ComTech, the attitude in this space was one of intensity; an expansive, highly competent community singularly focused on a monetary goal. Its pulsing energy vibrated my very marrow.

Shown to a conference room, I was seized by terror as I surveyed the seven men and women, all readied for battle, seated in an arc facing me. In the semi-trance of war, I shielded myself from their rocks and arrows and fired back with equal artillery. When the meeting concluded, I was met with appreciative nods. I would live to tell this tale.

Though portions of the day's rigors were similar in fashion to those met in my previous interviews, the flavor was different; less smiling, less warmth, more observation. This interview was intricately designed and carefully orchestrated, my every movement, every action, every response catalogued. These people weren't playing around.

At three-thirty, I was delivered to a large office that was in all ways intimidating. The room was sleek—all metal and glass, much like the exterior of the building itself. The soaring view through the wall of windows made my head swim.

With nearly silent footfalls, a man

entered the room. The silver streaks subtly woven through his dark suit matched those threading his hair. Though handsome in ways I'd never considered, it was his radiating power that drew my eyes to his.

"Good afternoon, Miss Wade," he said softly. His voice held a silken quality that was nearly hypnotic. We shook hands, and he motioned towards a modern-styled black leather chair before taking his own. He glanced cursorily at my resume, and then set it aside.

"Com-puter...business...Northwestern. *Hmm*." His chiseled face was the picture of calm inquisitiveness as he met my eyes once again. "I didn't notice many extracurriculars."

My stomach clenched. I had a great explanation and some stuff that vaguely resembled philanthropy. For example, I regularly left bits of hamburger meat for this mangy stray cat that hung around the restaurant's dumpsters. That equated to "animal rescue volunteer" in my mind. Then there was the time I gave a dollar to this rag-clad derelict in the train station. That surely counted for "working with the homeless", right?

"*Weyulla*—" In horror, I brutally focused on my accent—my *non-*accent. He raised his hand to silence me.

"How many hours per week do you work?"

I blinked convulsively. "Huh?"

His lips twitched. "Your resume says you have a job."

"Yes, that is correct."

"How many hours per week do you typically work?"

"Thirty—more if necessary."

"When do you have time for your stacked academic load?"

"I don't get a lot of sleep," I replied, chuckling. He cocked his head slightly and placidly looked at me—my eyes, nothing else.

Finally, he spoke. "INTech doesn't value sleep as a general rule. What is your position?" I was becoming flustered. I fully expected him to discuss my GPA, my choice of majors, where I wanted to be in the next X years—the standard. I was completely ready for all that stuff, but this...?

"You've stated that you work in a café. Are you a barista?" My thoughts turned to Brittney, the sheer mockery of a barista, and how easy her job was, how top-shelf. I shook my head no.

He steepled his fingers. "Then what is your position?"

"I'm the night manager. The restaurant is called *Burger Hut* Café. It's a glorified diner that stays open until...well, until all the customers leave. I manage a fry-cook and a waitress, when we have one. I take orders, serve food, clean up, lock up, and deliver the night's earnings to the bank."

"Hmm. When you say 'clean up', what exactly does that entail?" *What a bizarre question!* Normally, I wouldn't be the least bit embarrassed about what I did, but in front of this picture of success, this perfectly manicured specimen of urbanity, I felt, well...inadequate.

"Miss Wade?"

I dropped my shoulders, resigned to the truth. "By 'clean up', I mean empty the grease traps, wipe down the kitchen and dining area, take out the garbage, mop the floors, scrub the bathrooms—that kind of stuff."

"It sounds rather unpleasant. Surely there are other, more *glamorous* jobs available. In fact, why work at all?" He elegantly raised a brow.

He was judging me—mocking me, even, looking down on me because I didn't have a "pretty" job, because I didn't wipe my forehead and sigh every time I had to pour a flipping cup of coffee. I suddenly thought of how welcoming ComTech had been, and that I already had a position waiting for me there, so as disastrous as it might be, I said what I felt.

"Northwestern is an elite and very expensive school. You may also note that I have a partial academic scholarship. *Partial.* I don't come from money, Mr. Philips. I took this job because I needed it, and because they pay me under the table and give me extra hours when I ask, and because I know how to work hard to get what I want." I hopped to my feet. "My future is what I care about, whether it's with INTech or elsewhere!"

My fists were clenched and I stayed my trembling lips with my teeth. I knew I had just destroyed my crystal opportunity to work for the greatest company on the planet. I'd just smashed it into shattering shards. I stared down at the floor, wondering if I had any chance of gluing it back together, or if he would simply ask me to leave. Wincing, I slowly met his eyes again.

The brows on his otherwise emotionless face rose slightly, and then he walked around the table, seating himself on the edge. His socks were clearly silk, and his shoes...I had no estimate of their brand or cost. After a moment, he said, "Mine was with Pizza Emporium. Same job, different food group." Smiling ruefully, he shook his head and laughed. "One night, I chased a guy three blocks to get back the tip he stole. It was a dollar."

My eyebrows nearly left my face.

"INTech isn't interested in your past, Miss Wade. We're interested in your drive, your work ethic, and your determination."

I exhaled perhaps the largest amount of spent air my lungs had ever held and smiled genuinely.

Standing again, he said, "It's been very...refreshing meeting you." He firmly shook my hand before escorting me to the door where his secretary had materialized.

"Brooke, please show Miss Wade to her four o'clock."

"Certainly, sir," she replied, beaming at him.

As we started down the corridor, he called out, "One more question." Fearfully, I whipped my head around. "Why is it called a 'café'?"

I melted, unable to hide my smile. "Because the owners think it sounds glamorous." His laughter followed him back into his office.

Quite honestly, the remainder of the day was a blur, and though I had other meetings and theoretically gave smart, coherent answers, I remained in a stunned state, locked in that pivotal, almost surreal moment when I realized that anyone, no matter how humble their beginnings, could become someone truly impressive, important, polished. I was now certain I could fulfill my mother's wish and become that very image. Nothing else mattered, or even held relevance.

II

Etiquette Lessons

"Scotch, neat," my dinner escort said to the bartender, as we waited for our table. He was a regional computer service representative. His title sounded quite important, and I was both impressed and grateful that he wasn't a salesperson. "What would you like, Susan?"

I had no flipping clue "what I'd like". I only knew that beer wasn't appropriate in this elegant setting.

Glancing around frantically, my eyes fell upon a group of businesswomen drinking a beautiful pale pink liquid from long-stemmed, conical glasses. "I'll have one of those," I said, pointing.

"Cosmopolitan," the bartender announced absently, placing the drink in front of me.

Inhaling before I took a sip, the slightly fruity fumes were enough to knock over a horse. I tried not to cough as the liquid seared my throat. My stomach was immediately filled with a soothing warmth. Holding this glass in my hand, I'd never felt so mature in my life.

"Are you a fan of sushi?" Richard asked when we were seated. His general demeanor seemed open and friendly, but based on the day's events, I was absolutely positive I was still being interviewed. Though exhausted, I kept my back straight and stayed fully alert.

Sushi was made with raw fish—that much I knew, but little was consumed in the South that wasn't cooked to the falling apart stage. As a college student, I mostly ate pizza or whatever was left over at Burger Hut, so my overall culinary experiences were fairly limited. I replied with a vague nod, and his lips twitched.

"Since I'm familiar with the menu here, shall I order?" He met my eyes and nodded slowly. I nodded slowly in return.

"That would be lovely, thank you." He smiled approvingly.

Determined not to make a fool of myself, I studied his every move. After briefly rubbing two bamboo sticks together, he positioned them in the crook of his thumb and gracefully manipulated them with pinched fingers.

"This is sashimi. I prefer it to sushi, proper. Lacking rice to dull the taste, I find the flavor richer. Don't you?"

"Of course," I replied, nodding faux-sagely.

"Please eat. You must be starving."

I readied my weapons of mass gastronomic destruction, and after praying to the ghost of Julia Child, carefully replicated his performance. Summoning Lexi-like focus, I lifted the first piece of translucent meat from the plate, and with a tremoring hand, successfully placed it in my mouth. I smiled as I chewed the oddly velvety salmon, pretending it was anything other than fishing bait.

"Octopus?" he offered next. The thick white disc had a rubbery consistency, but I managed, chasing it quickly with a healthy gulp of alcohol. Finally he said, "Eel is my favorite. It's so flavorful, don't you think?"

"Absolutely." Internally, I cringed, but the smile never left my face. People ate snake in the Wild West and lived, I reasoned. I'd always heard it tasted like chicken—of course, everything gross and disgusting supposedly tastes like chicken. Putting those thoughts aside, I decided right then and there that I would eat this brown, gooey-looking chunk of sea creature, and hold his eyes the whole time. He was playing chicken with me—*pun intended*—and I was going to win.

Though a little fatty in texture, the flavor was...quite amazing. He offered me the last piece on the small platter, and I reached for it without a word. His lips turned up at the corners. I would learn to love this dish they called sushi. I would make it my personal favorite.

"How was your flight?" he asked pleasantly.

"Very uneventful," I replied with the casual shrug of a seasoned traveler whose plane had not crashed.

Richard nodded to someone behind me, and a waiter appeared at our table, holding a burgundy, leather-bound book in his arms.

"Wine?" he asked.

Richard inclined his head towards me.

The only wine I'd ever tasted had come from a bottle Felicia Jones had lifted from her parents' liquor cabinet in the tenth grade. We'd sat in the woods behind her house, passing the bottle back and forth, grimacing at what tasted very much like strawberry cough syrup.

"Yes, please." My cosmopolitan was replaced by a wineglass as Richard perused the menu.

"Do you have a preference?" *Another test.*

"The sushi—sashimi, I mean, was wonderful. I'd love it if you'd choose the wine as well."

He swirled and sniffed and tasted, and then a small portion was delivered to each of our bulbous glasses. I followed his every move. This, too, I must learn. The dark, brooding wine must have been wonderful, since he savored it like chocolate. I pretended to do the same.

"Tell me truthfully," he said, eyes

gleaming, "do you prefer Argentinian or Chilean Malbacs?"

Heaven help me! The only two places I was aware wine was produced were France and California.

I took a deep, cleansing breath. "It depends," I answered.

He hesitated for a moment, and then said, "I agree."

Dinner was next. While reviewing the confusing descriptions, I balked at the prices. Most entrees were a full week's salary, and I felt the urgent need to choose the least expensive out of sheer politeness. After all, INTech had already paid for my flight, a gorgeous hotel room, and who the hell knows how much this wine cost.

"I'm a steak fan. How about you?" he said after a moment.

I sagged with gratitude and nodded.

"The prime rib is fabulous here." He raised his eyebrows in question.

"You order, I'll eat." His eyes twinkled, and I wasn't sure why, but rather than tested, I suddenly felt I'd graduated. I smiled broadly as he signaled our waiter.

The plane ride home went much like the evening. With newfound confidence, I'd whipped off my shoes at the correct time and found my gate with little effort. I felt officially grown up now; a real professional.

12

Wanted Fugitive

I'd bitten my nails to the quick waiting for campus mail to arrive. Day
three and I was altogether panicked.
ComTech had provided a good package and a decent salary—the promise
of it, anyway, but I'd stood on the
mountain with Moses and glimpsed
the Promised Land.

The deadline on my calendar
stared sternly at me. If I didn't hear
from INTech today, I'd have to accept

my one-way ticket to Dallas and be grateful for it. It was a gift—any job right out of college was a gift. Perhaps Ben had been right all along. It was foolish to throw away a real job for a pipedream. *But the majesty of it...*

Starved, I slurped ramen noodles from a mug as I stared at the phone, wrestling with my angst, tapping my foot impatiently. *Oh fuck it!* I tore out of the room to check the mail one last time.

There was nothing in my box. I slapped the best smile I owned on my face and nodded. *ComTech it is.*

Marching through the deserted post office with a sense of newfound purpose, I tripped over an express package lying on the floor. I'd been tripping over them for weeks now. Too large to fit in our tiny mailboxes, the workers habitually dumped them on the floor like rubbish to be trampled upon. Futures were at stake—lives sprouted from these very parcels. Unfounded hope flared, and I frantically snatched up the packet and checked the name; someone else's soiled dream.

I wandered back to my dorm in a semi-trance, my emotions riding a twisting rollercoaster. I had a good life ahead—no, a great one! I took a cleansing breath and reached for the phone to cement my future. It rang loudly and slipped from my grasp. Fumbling for it, I dropped to my knees.

"Hello?"

"May I speak with Susan Wade?" The voice sounded out of sorts, and I assumed it was ComTech ready to rip me a new one for not calling sooner—or the bank. It could always be the bank.

Summoning an explanation, I cringed and said, "This is...she?"

"Excellent. This is Natasha Cummings, Human Resources Manager for INTech Corporation. We met last week when you interviewed." Beating wildly, my heart leapt into my throat. "I'm calling to follow up on the offer we made you. I assume, by now, you've read over the packet. Do you have any questions?"

"Um—"

"It's our standard salary and benefits package for entry-level computer service representatives."

I was speechless, except for the weird gurgling noise I couldn't seem to control.

"Our company is *very* discerning, Miss Wade, and we only make offers to a select few. But when we do choose a candidate, we expect results. You understand this."

"Yes," I breathed. "Of course."

Just then, Lexi stormed into the room and screamed, "Fucking bitch!" at the top of her lungs.

Horrified, I waved frantically, pantomiming that this was the single most important call of my life. She rolled her eyes and held up a large, oddly-stained, express envelope, INTech's imprint clearly shining on the label. Already opened, the smudged and wrinkled contents appeared to have been crammed back inside. My vision blurred with molten rage.

"Miss Wade?"

"Sorry," I replied, closing my eyes to shut out the festering haze. As I inhaled a lung-splitting breath to quell my fury, the most bizarre thing happened: my education kicked in. *Leverage!*

"Forgive my delay in responding." I felt quite faint, but plowed forward. "I have another offer on the table that I'm weighing."

"Oh? May I ask whose?"

"ComTech's," I replied lightheadedly.

"When is your deadline?"

"Honestly, I intend to make my decision today." *No lie there.*

"What would sway you in our direction?" Her tone took on a competitive edge, and I couldn't believe my ears. Without a chance to review INTech's material, I had no strategic answer—not that I truly needed one.

Before I uttered a sound, she asked, "Would you be willing to give us an hour?"

"Yes," I croaked, praying I hadn't screwed up.

"Expect a call at one o'clock. Perhaps we can 'value-add' a little."

"That would be awe—lovely. I look forward to your call."

I hung up and jumped to my feet, my fists clenched in rage. "What the hell, Lexi?! This was *mine!*"

"No shit. It was lying on the mail-room floor. I didn't know whose it was until that bitch, Brittney Cox, ripped it open and started reading it to her pack of whores. It was weird. When she got past the 'Dear Miss Wade' part, her face went totally white."

"I'll kill her!" I screamed.

"No need." Lexi's smile was at least two-thousand watts. "Good thing my dad's a lawyer. I might be calling him later."

My eyes traveled down her ripped clothing. I'd assumed this was her wardrobe nightmare of the day, until I noticed blood on her knuckles and a blazing skinned knee through her torn fishnets. I looked up in shock.

Just then, a resounding knock rattled the door. "Alexis Stiles?" said a commanding male voice. "Open the door."

My eyes bulged.

"Stall 'em," she whispered, wrenching open the window. I tossed her backpack to her as she slid out, and then quickly dropped the blinds. Crossing the room calmly, I opened the door.

"May I help you?" The large campus police officer looked up after glancing at his notepad, and narrowed his eyes.

"Are you Alexis Stiles?"

"No, I'm her roommate."

"So you are..." He looked again at his notepad. "Susan Wade?"

"Yes."

"Is she here?"

Very clearly excited to have something to do other than dole out parking tickets, his eyes danced, and I feared for my darling, Goth warrior. I swept my arm across the small and ugly pen in which we lived and shook my head no.

"When did you last see her?"

"Why? Is she okay?! Bless her little heart, she works so hard, studyin' 'til late at night. And I'm always worried somethin's gonna happen to her. She's so fragile and innocent, and there are some *mean* people on this campus. Are y'all aware of that?" I asked in a scolding tone. "And then I work super long hours, too—I'm double majorin' in business and computer technology, ya know. And I've been out interviewin' a lot lately and—"

I hit him with a churning river of utterly useless information, my Southern accent barreling down on him like a freight train loaded with elongated vowels and consonant combinations that don't actually exist in the modern English language. He tried to interrupt several times, but I'd found my pace like a revival preacher on a saving binge.

Finally, he looked heavenward and shoved a card in my hand as I continued reciting the names, numbers, and home addresses of my employer, my parents and anyone else I could think of.

"Call this number if you see her."

"Okaaya," I said, chasing him

down the hall. "But I didn't tell yew 'bout my dawg named Leroy. My daddy had to put him to sleep and I cried and I—" The door slammed behind him and I fell on the floor, cackling. *Poor Lexi.*

Still chuckling, I rifled through the large stack of embossed papers until I found the itemized salary and benefits page. When I read it, I gasped in awe, and decided Brittney, bail money, and breathing in general were no longer important.

At one o'clock sharp the ring stopped my heart.

"Miss Wade, INTech is willing to offer a five-thousand dollar signing bonus if you accept today. If not, the entire offer is void. It's your choice."

A great sense of perfect peace settled over me. "I'll take it."

"Excellent. Please contact *Moving*

Services. You'll find their number on page two. When do you graduate?"

"May eighth," I responded through the shimmering ether.

"Excellent. You'll begin your training in Philadelphia on May eleventh."

"Wow, that's really...fast."

"We don't waste time or resources. Our next quarterly meeting occurs at the end of May. You'll receive your job assignment then."

"I'll be there on the eleventh."

"I look forward to seeing you again. Oh, and Miss Wade?"

"Yes?"

"Congratulations. You're the newest member of the INTech family."

And that is when I wet myself...

U

I didn't race from the room, climb the central clock tower, and shout my victory to the masses, as one might expect. Rather, I lay back, closed my eyes, and basked in the aura of blessed grace. This was what my entire life had been leading up to. This very moment. The golden chalice that held a certain and bountiful future was now in my grasp. I sighed in undiluted ecstasy and drifted into oblivion.

"Should I call 911?" Lexi asked, flipping on the overhead light.

Shielding my eyes, I jumped to my feet. "Lexi! Are you okay?" I whispered frantically. "Did they arrest you?"

"It's cool. Daddy made a call."

I gawked in horror. "But, but you have a criminal record now!"

"*Seriously?*" She rolled her eyes. "It's just stupid campus police. It's not like they're real. Besides," she said, her sour smirk morphing into a rare and beatific smile, "turns out, tampering with mail is a federal offense. Now let's go get wasted!"

Brimming with unearthly jubilation, I grabbed Lexi's arm and raced to the door. But then my sad sense of responsibility kicked in. "What time is it?"

"Eleven."

"Holy shit! I'm way late for work."

"No you're not."

"What do you—of course I am!"

She broke into yet another smile—this one sly and befitting. "I called in for you. Evidently, you have some kind of twenty-four hour flu.

Puking your brains out. It's disgusting."

I squealed as we swept across the commons like demented leprechauns, laughing and dancing on the tables of every fraternity house on campus. By four a.m., I *was* puking my brains out, and I spent the next two hours with my face warming the blessedly chilled tiles of the hall's communal bathroom.

"I'm gonna die," I said, withering on the keyboard.

"Is it contagious?" Ben asked, quickly stepping back.

I looked at him through a single bleary eye. "Is a hangover contagious?"

Relaxing, he chuckled then pinched his nose. "You need a shower."

"Ya think?"

"So...what happened last night? The Burger Hut guy said you were sick."

"Do I not look sick to you?"

He snorted, but then furrowed his brow. "Why didn't...you could have called me." He made a huffing sound. "I would have come with you. I mean, we're, you know, like...well, dating."

I didn't reply with any number of things running through my mind, one very large point being we *weren't* dating. Instead, I just smiled gloriously and said, "I got a job!"

"You accepted with ComTech? *Yes!*" He fist-pumped the air in his usual style.

"No, I turned them down. You're

looking at INTech Corporation's newest addition," I announced loud enough for the entire class to hear. Heads whipped around, and the gasps that exploded from the jealous and the awestruck were a moving symphony.

Brittney narrowed her piercing blue eyes—well, the one that was fully open, and I glared back, enjoying my own brand of vengeance.

"What?!" Ben whispered heatedly. "INTech *hired* you?"

"Yes," I said, proudly raising my chin. "Yes, they did."

His ruddy eyebrows crinkled, and he looked truly hurt. "I thought we were gonna be roomies and stuff."

"Ben—"

"I gotta go." Sliding his laptop into his grungy green backpack, he left mid-class.

13

Geek Dogfood

The swivel stool that had become Ben's was currently occupied by an unmistakably freshman blob loudly slurping a milkshake. Every time the door opened, I glanced anxiously, but Ben never showed. I felt no guilt for not fulfilling his lopsided fantasy, but punishing me wouldn't fix anything. I had my own life to live, and he his.

After work, I knocked on his dorm room door. Sure, it was late, but this was college. *Who actually slept?* His roommate opened the door and smiled in an *oh hell, yeah* kind of way. I glanced at his snowman boxers and snorted. "Is Ben here?"

"Nope, but I am."

"Yes, Tommy, I am aware that you are here, as I can plainly see you. Do you know where he is?"

"You can wait for him. You want a beer?"

I shook my head. "Could you please tell him I stopped by."

"You're alone. I'm alone. We could fix that little problem."

I rolled my eyes. "Call me when you get your braces off," I said, turning away.

"I can't believe this is your last day," Mr. Bellman said, giving me an awkward hug. His wife, Margie, did the same, and then dabbed her eyes.

"Me neither," I sniffled as I handed him my disgusting apron.

"Keep it as a souvenir. You know, to remember us by."

I wrinkled my nose, but forced a smile. His heart was in the right place. "Thanks. Don't worry, I'll never forget you."

"Four years," he marveled, shaking his head. "I remember when you were a freshman, all nervous and trying to do a good job. Now look at you! You're calm and confident—a real career woman in the making. You're gonna do great things, Susan. Great things. Isn't that right, Margie?" She nodded, blew her nose, and then thrust him an envelope, which he then handed to me. He looked at the floor and shuffled his feet.

"It's not much, really, but it'll help you get started. And we—" he looked at his wife and squeezed her shoulder. "Well, you've been like a daughter to us."

I pulled out the card signed by all the employees, and after reading the sentiment, nearly dropped it. "This will help a lot," I murmured, staring at the two one-hundred dollar bills tucked inside. I threw myself against them. "Thank you so much!"

"We're so proud of you," they said in unison.

I wasn't exactly sure how this would go over, but I thought, why not? After so many years, they'd sort of become my loud, heavy-set, Midwestern relatives as well. "Mr. and Mrs. Bellman, I don't know if you have plans, but my graduation ceremony is Friday, and I have these two tickets." I pulled them from my backpack. "My parents can't come, and I was wondering if maybe, you'd like to, maybe...take their place?"

They stared at me for a moment in mild shock, and then looked at each other, their smiles radiant. "Oh sweetheart, we'd love to come!" Margie said, hugging me fiercely and then blowing her nose again.

I began choking up as well, feeling altogether less abandoned. "Okay, great. Well, I've got some packing to do. I'll see you Friday."

"You betcha," Mr. Bellman said.

This place was a gungy, aged hole, and the job exhausting and basically thankless, but the owners and their kindness—that I would miss. I took one last long glance around the room, waved enthusiastically to my substitute parents, and left the Burger Hut Café forever.

U

There was no reason not to skip across the quad with a light heart. The flowers were blooming—*finally*, the birds were chirping, and I was half a centimeter shy of bursting into song.

"Ben!" I yelled, waving. Deep in conversation with a tall blonde that looked exceedingly like Brittney, he pressed his lanky body against hers and kissed her cheek. I gasped for air. This could not be happening! As I raced towards them, debating which one to hit, I decided at the last moment to simply scream, "*Ew!*"

Ben turned and forced a smile. "Hello, Susan. Do you know Sandra?"

"Of course, I know Sandra," I said, relieved at least that it wasn't the witch. "She's been in every computer class we've ever taken! How are you, Sandra?"

"Hi, Susan, I'm great, I got a job with ComTech, I'm moving to Texas," she said robotically, bobbing up and down as she waved furiously. She pushed her oversized, black-framed glasses up the bridge of her nose and looked up at Ben, all doe-eyed.

"I missed you last night. I wanted to talk to you," I said to Ben.

"Yeah, I was kinda busy." He smiled at Sandra then draped his arm over her shoulders. She giggled in a dorky, computer geeky kind of way.

"I also dropped by your room at three this morning and you weren't there, either." Then my dimly lit candle flared. I looked from one to the other. "You spent the night with her? What the heck?" So what if I'd failed to induce real feelings for him? He was *my* lab partner, *my* coffee buddy, *my* stalker, dammit!

He blushed furiously, but set his chin. "I'll be in Dallas and you'll be in Philly. Us dating doesn't make sense."

"Wait! You're breaking up with me?"

"Sorry, Susan, Sandra and I are together now. But can we be, like, friends?" Nodding furiously, Sandra looked genuinely earnest.

"No, we can't be 'like' friends, you dumb shit! We can't be 'like' anything!" I spat out, and then stormed across the grass.

This was literally the story of my life continuing to play out as it always had. I'd been in love, I'd been in lust, and with Ben, I'd even been in kinda, sorta, maybe like. Regardless, it ended the same way every time—them breaking up with me. I swear, for just once, I'd like to be the one who did the breaking up, the one who didn't get blindsided. In fact, this was going to be the day!

I turned on my heels and strode back to the happy geek couple, who would have a geek wedding and geek children and geek cars, and would adopt geek pets with stupid skin allergies that would have to eat weird, organic, geek dog food.

"You know what, Ben? I'm glad that you have Sandra and Texas and really great tacos in your future, but I don't care! I'll be in an amazing city with amazing people, working for an amazing company, driving an amazing car. And I'll have an amazing boyfriend, who also has an amazing car *and* power *and* money and knows how to wipe his damn mouth when he eats!" I screeched. "So, so...I'm breaking up with *you*!" I poked his chest with my finger, stomped on his foot, and marched off, feeling fully vindicated...*and* pretty darn happy for him.

14

Martin Luther King

Exams were over, grades had been assigned, and I'd achieved my goals—every one of them. I crossed the commons in a state of great satisfaction. Next week I would be in Philadelphia, beginning my new life. After four grueling years, this place would no longer be my home. And then it suddenly hit me: today was my very last day as a college student.

I stared through new eyes at my

familiar surroundings: that bush beside the bookstore shaped like a deformed puffer fish, the trees we rolled with stolen toilet paper whenever Northwestern won a ball game, these broad student union stairs I'd slipped down my freshman year, landing me right on my butt in front of the entire lacrosse team. I lovingly ran my hand up the railing, gazing at the chiseled archway above. I might never see this meaningless frieze again. My eyes misted.

I had one more goodbye to deliver—this one tainted with mixed feelings. With a sudden sense of sacred ritual, I somberly stepped to the counter in front of my faithful enemy.

"A latte, please."

Brittney stood motionless, eyebrows in defensive position, snide remark on the runway. I tilted my head and simply took her in. She was no longer the somewhat intimidating creature under whose shadow of popularity I'd lived for four years. She was simply a silly girl trying to forge a life for herself, just like me. And knowing she'd be working for a company that would most likely bleed every drop of happiness from her life, I felt a twinge of sympathy for her—a *tiny* twinge.

"*Just* a latte?" she asked warily.

"Just a latte."

"No tricks?"

I solemnly shook my head. "None."

Turning away slowly, she almost looked disappointed, and I realized it was thoroughly unkind, and quite frankly, disappointingly anti-climactic to part on such terms. I waited until she poured the milk, and then counted to three. "Soy, grande, iced, sugar-free, vanilla latte."

She let out the mighty groan she'd been saving just for me, glared furiously over her shoulder, and tried very hard, I noticed, not to smile. After wiping her brow, she forcefully slid the drink across the counter with a vengeful scowl. "I hate you, you know."

"So?"

"I saw your letter from INTech. You're getting a salary," she hissed.

"So are you."

Appearing to war with herself, she shifted on her feet and sullenly stared at the laminate countertop. Then she huffed loudly and met my eyes. "ComSync's not paying me."

"What do you mean? I thought you said you had a *real* job."

"It is a *real* job. It's what ComSync offers people right out of college. I'll get tons of experience, and then later..." Tears welled in her eyes. I waited patiently for her to pull herself back together. "It's just the unpaid internship kind of real job," she finally mumbled.

"Brittney, why did you take it?"

"Because, because...it's my best chance for a job! I don't have the kind of GPA a loser like you has. I didn't live in the library every waking moment of my day. I had friends, a boyfriend, a social life. I did stuff. Grades weren't everything, you know!"

"Until now."

"Yeah," she muttered. "Until now."

Though feeling no guilt whatever, I pulled out my wallet and stuffed five *very* hard-earned dollars in her tip jar. After a moment of intense eye-contact that conveyed all the things we could never civilly say to one another, she nodded.

"Nice knowing ya, Brittney," I said, saluting her.

She raised an eyebrow, and her lips twitched, but then she turned the full force of her evil glare on me. "Next!" she wailed.

Sipping syrupy coffee, I chuckled all the way back to my dorm. Though I'd relished wallowing in my hatred towards Brittney these last four years, I would not understand the true meaning of that word for nearly a decade. Only in my darkest future would I be capable of looking some-one straight in the eye, and with all the certainty in the Universe, know that I could watch them bleed to death at my feet without a trace of remorse. No, it would be a long time before I felt such things. But I would.

U

Lexi had been sullen and snippy all morning as we feverishly finished packing. I shimmied into my outfit and slipped on my tan heels. "Why aren't your parents here, yet?" I finally asked.

"Why aren't yours?" she shot back.

My lips began trembling and tears welled. "They're not coming," I whispered. "It's too far to drive, my dad's a jerk, and my mom's, my mom's—" Fracturing, I crumbled onto my bed and sobbed uncontrollably, unable to hold back the epic flood of bitterness and utter resentment any longer. After what seemed an hour, I felt a hand tenderly stroking my hair and realized it belonged to Lexi.

"Stop crying, Susan," she said softly. "Shake it off and be done with it." And then in a tone encrusted with the same bitterness and resentment I felt: "My parents aren't coming either. Dad's out of the country on business, and when I texted Mom a picture of my new tattoo, she said she was too embarrassed to be seen with me. Fuck her."

I smiled a little at that. "Yeah, fuck her, Lexi. Fuck her. Fuck him. Fuck them all!" I sat up, and after giving her suddenly stiff body a big hug, I clasped her shoulders and looked into her heavily kohl shaded eyes. "You and I—we can't depend on anyone but ourselves. But we are strong.

We will do great things. We shall overcome!"

"You sound like fucking Martin Luther King," she said in a thick voice, a wobbly smile floating on her lips.

"We're graduating from college, dammit. Let's have a toast!" I scrambled off my bare mattress and pulled out the shiny bottle of champagne hidden behind my junky suitcase. "I bought this as your graduation gift, and to say thanks for the suit." My own smile wavered as I again thought of what she had done for me.

"Open it!" she ordered, scuttling to her stack of boxes. She rifled through several before pulling out two Northwestern University crest embossed shot glasses.

The cork exploded, ricocheting off the far wall, and foam spewed down my graduation dress, soaking my lap. Laughing, I decided it really didn't matter.

"To overcoming!" I shouted, raising my glass.

"To fucking Martin Luther King!" she returned.

I snorted as we tapped thimbles.

"Yeah, Lexi, to fucking Martin Luther King."

The End of Book 1

Thank you for reading The Interview. *I truly hope you enjoyed meeting young Susan Wade. This is merely the beginning of her epic journey through the corporate jungle. As INTech molds her into its own evil image, she will become a very different woman. She'll suffer great tragedy, divorce herself from decency and kindness, and eventually know heartbreaking joy. She's waiting for you in* The

Carrot: Book 2 of the Susan Wade Saga

The Carrot - Sample

Holy crap! Two weeks ago, I was blissfully enjoying my fairly perfect life. Now I've just boarded a plane to Hell—the real one, with the heat and the desperation and the...what *is* that smell? And it's not even my fault—well, not technically, anyway...

As the plane pierced the cloudbank, the tone chimed, and a disinterested, yet cheerful voice explained that the *Fasten Seat Belt* sign had been turned off and it was now safe to fire up every electronic device you'd ever owned. An aside: It is my firm and sincere belief that *Angry Birds* will not bring down a 737.

Racing against every other business person on board, I pulled out my laptop and began flipping through client accounts. My boss wasn't kidding when he said the eastern region—*my* shitty new region—was a difficult place to grow business. At least I knew why.

You see, I was born Southern, raised Southern...but I did not want to be Southern. I simply wanted to be Susan; Susan Wade of some random, non-controversial, non-embarrassing place. So I left, quite literally. I didn't climb out my window and run away from home, though I'd tried several times. No, I bided my time, planned and plotted, took all the necessary measures.

And when the opportunity presented itself, I afforded a single sidelong glance to the sleepy, mist-encircled Pilot Mountain—the megalith looming over my entire existence, and made my thrilling escape to Chicago, racing from heritage and homeland to an unexplored, but surely more enlightened harbor.

After crossing the Mason-Dixon Line—*for the first time in my whole entire life!*—I tossed the last of Mom's country ham biscuits out the window and laughed maniacally. Okay, what really happened is this: I totally freaked, pulled to the side of the interstate, and hurled up said biscuits. While on all fours I finished the job properly by purging terms including, but not limited to *y'all*, *ain't*, *hey*, and anything ending in *in'*. The soil absorbed them hungrily.

Determined to successfully graft, I'd studied this Northern species; its culture, mannerisms, and customs. Mimic. Infiltrate. Become. And, as I skimmed the outskirts of this vast city, I reviewed my crucial list: do not wave, do not converse with random strangers, do not make direct eye-contact in elevators or enclosed spaces—it makes them uncomfortable, do not freely smile, and for God's sake, do NOT hug anybody!

My tribe is a friendly lot that openly studies one another, judges by appearance, then slaughters piously. As for smiling, I didn't do it all that often anyway, and bruised purple on the inside, I rarely wrapped my arms around anything other than my mid-section unless forced by that ominous creature known only as "Mother". Though daunting, in the end, abandoning Southern tradition was simply part of the decontamination process; a re-tooling of body and brain to perform in a novel fashion; the price paid for admittance to the new world.

Northwestern University was a mad mix of people from the other three-quarters of the country; my clean slate; my opportunity to convince those around me that I was someone to be taken seriously, someone special...someone who did not *need* others!

Having grown up all too aware that need was the Devil's road to slavery, and slavery to bone-crushing heartache, I made it my single-minded mission to become self-reliant. And to that end, I set to the task of developing a steel core of self-discipline, earning me top grades in both my majors. And if missing parties, skipping football games, and avoiding serious relationships was the price of success, then so be it.

Four years later when I left Chicago, parchment diploma in hand, I'd emerged from my chrysalis a liberated, sanctimoniously free-thinking person, completely cleansed of all things Southern; a woman with an extraordinary career lying at her feet; a woman en route to that shimmering city called Philadelphia.

And I dove headfirst into its glimmering ocean of urbanity, learning to swim through its gridlocks of hostile motorists, evade its tow truck operators who, like hungry sharks, skulked at every corner poised to whisk my car to scary impound lots, and, though scoring my ethical peel, feed on its indifference. It was the only way to survive.

After a shot-gun wedding to INTech Corporation, one of the largest Internet technology companies in the world, I plunged into its corporate sea with the same zeal. Here, at its world headquarters, open hostility took the polished forms of intimidation and manipulation, the lurking sharks were far better dressed...but the indifference was exactly the same.

Now a sage at twenty-nine, having grown talons for clawing and sharp teeth for biting, I was a great deal meaner, significantly more jaded, and rarely forgiving of those who got in my way. I was also tremendously sophisticated, wholly independent, and thoroughly exhausted most of the time. And I loved this grown-up Susan. And I loved my all-consuming career. And I loved my life just the way it was, dammit!

The crux: I was hungry, and maybe a little greedy, though I certainly didn't see it that way at the time.

The invitation to fill my belly came one crisp winter morning, hand-delivered by my closest ally and self-appointed champion, The District Manager of Rhode Island. Taking form beside me, her face gleamed with smug pleasure as she announced, "We've had a break-through."

"Oh?"

"The posting's been out five seconds. This is the one!"

When not busy shredding her

underlings to bits, Kirsten tirelessly searched for ways—alleyways—to get me promoted. She knew it was all in the world I wanted, but my work ethic, faith in perseverance, and professional dedication was simply farce to her.

During my short career, I'd already risen to an important position within the corporation; a highly-rated regional service representative. In company terms, I negotiated and vended computer service agreements and eradicated both technical and software interface issues. In layman's terms, I cajoled people into buying service contracts and then fixed their computers. I was quite good at my job...but my job wasn't quite good enough for me.

"North Carolina!" She whispered

the words as if they were magic. They were—the black kind.

"N-North Carolina?!" I sputtered, choking. "Did you say *North* Carolina?" The concept defied words.

"Susan, you've got to take risks if you want to move up. Surely you realize that." She stopped suddenly and scowled at the secretary, arms full of paper, who dared hesitate at the copier nearest us.

"Of course I do," I snapped, glowering over her shoulder at a world she could not see. "But not *there!*"

That was bomb number one. She had a pocketful that day.

"I've already spoken to Bob on your behalf, and he loves the idea." She smiled as if she'd moved heaven and earth. She had—mine!

"You what?!" I squeaked incredulously. "How could you do that without speaking with me first?"

Kirsten dismissed my outburst with an elegant wave. "You would have said no, and *no* won't get you promoted, hun. Your meeting's at one-thirty. You'll thank me later. Ta!" And with that she turned on her heels, leaving me gasping.

"Ta" about summed it up, too, because regardless of my protests, feet-stamping, and the rather embarrassing tantrum I'd thrown at lunch that day, here I was, hurtling at some high velocity towards this terrifying destination. And by my own doing...*sort of.*

"WADE!" Bob Shillings, Senior Vice President of the Eastern US Retail Service Division, known simply as *God Almighty* to us peons, bellowed down the hall that same afternoon.

I was scared shitless of the man, and rightly so. Why, you might ask? Because, other than holding my career—aka world—by its whiskers, he wasn't actually my boss; he was my boss' boss' boss. Beth Stamler, my *now-on-maternity-leave-having-thoughtlessly-left-me-in-the-hands-of-the-likes-of-this-man* district manager was my immediate supervisor. Hers was a vice president who'd been loaned out on "special assignment"—whatever that meant. So, as of now, there was nothing but thin air between the two of us.

As I scampered to *Mount Olympus*, I passed "Strategy Girl". Kirsten gave me an enthusiastic thumbs-up. I glared back, seriously weighing the merits of flipping her off.

"Shut the door," he said, failing to look up from his computer screen. "I'm surprised you requested this assignment. I don't usually send seasoned reps to low grossing areas." *Ha!* "Unfortunately, this project's become high exposure." He made a nasty face, but continued typing. "If you're successful there, you'll get noticed, so I can see the enticement. But know now, there's real downside if you aren't." *Not so* "Ha!"

"Oh," I softly responded, my Greek salad turning to leafy lead in my stomach.

"What's the problem with West Penn?"

For the last four years I'd run Pennsylvania's western region. It was a lucrative part of a fairly lucrative state, housing several substantial cities, including my crown jewel and part-time lover, Pittsburgh.

"No problem, Bob. I, I love West Penn," I stammered like an idiot. "I have a great sales team, my customer base is excellent, and—"

"As you've no doubt read between the lines, INTech, or rather *I* have a situation in North Carolina," he said, plowing over me in tyrannical style. "Problem seems to be public relations. It's a damn mess down there and I need it cleaned up." As he grimaced at his screen, I stood quietly, wondering if he'd notice if I bolted back down the hall.

"I've reviewed your records. You hit your numbers consistently. More to the point, you've had no customer complaints, and that's saying something." He shook his head succinctly.

"Overall, I'm pleased with your work."

"That's good to know, Bob," I responded feeling warily pleased.

"What I don't understand is your timing." He took off his thick-framed glasses and rubbed his eyes. "If you wanted a transfer, it could have been settled at Quarterlies last week when everyone was in town."

INTech's Quarterlies, a week-long affair occurring four times a year, summoned everyone to the Mother-ship for company-wide meetings, training seminars, re-organizations, promotions, etc. Oh, and transfers.

Bob looked up at me for the first time and I stared back blankly. Finally, he raised his eyebrows sharply and cleared his throat, and I realized he was waiting for some sort of explanation—one I didn't have. It wasn't like I could say "oops" to the man, and "Kirsten's making me do it" wasn't exactly going to fly either. So, I went with what I hoped sounded believable.

"Um, well, I've been considering my options for career advancement—*that part was true*—and this seemed like a unique line of approach." *"Unique"? Yeah, that was one word for it; "stupid" was another.* "If the timing's off, perhaps we should revisit this discussion before next Quarterlies." *There, that should get me out of this mess.*

Smiling at him with faux confidence, I squared my shoulders and waited for him to say something like "Fine. Go away." But after a moment of suffocating silence, he simply said, "I see." His eyes returned to his monitor and his fingers flew across the keyboard. Standing over him, I had a perfect aerial view of the top of his head. Freckled pink skin peeked through an interceding, mostly gray combover, and I wondered just how old he was.

"This region's particularly challenging for some reason," he finally continued. "But Kirsten tells me you grew up in Carolina." I opened my mouth and gulped for air like a caught fish.

Since joining the company, I'd carefully hidden my roots under a big rock, hoping that deprived of sunlight, they might just wither and die. My aim was to completely dissociate myself from the misconception that Southern girls are cute, but stupid; I was neither.

Familiar with the mask I wore, as with so many of my life's private details, Kirsten had used this little poison tidbit to leverage my—*her*—advantage. She hated losing. *Ever*. And though her brashness shouldn't have surprised me, for once, it did.

"Yes," I confessed, fidgeting with the paperclip I'd forgotten to toss before entering the sacred realm. *Born there, raised there, escaped from there, hoped never to return there.*

"Good. That means you speak 'Southern'." Abruptly, he stopped typing and his lips turned up in a fiendish grin I'm certain I'll never forget. He looked at me with eyes that had just seen clear to checkmate, and eased back in his loudly protesting chair.

"Alright, Wade. I'll send you to North Carolina. But, let's be clear; I want this region off my plate. *For.*

Good. Understand?" I smiled tightly, having absolutely no idea what he was talking about. "And as incentive, I'll make you a deal. A district manager position in the Midwest may open up later this year. If you increase numbers down there by, say...twenty percent over the next six months, I'll consider you for the slot. Agreed?" I nodded like a bobble-head doll, trying to hide my astonishment. *She was right!*

"In some ways I'm glad it's you who volunteered. You're competent. Maybe you can end this nightmare for me." His dreamy expression weirded me out almost as much as his *never-before-seen-by-human-eyes* smile.

Vacillating between sudden euphoria and abject terror, emphasis on the latter, I meekly asked, "Bob, since this assignment is only temporary, if I don't hit the twenty percent mark, can I assume I'll return to West Penn?"

"Susan, that's not how it works." After saying my actual first name, his bizarre expression faded, and he returned to his normal grumpy self. "No '*ifs*'. Get North Carolina fixed!"

"Right." I swallowed hard as a surge of vertigo hit me.

"You'll train your replacement next week—assuming I find one that fast," he grumbled under his breath. "Then you'll head south."

"So soon..." I whispered to myself. And then: "Dear God...this is really happening!"

"We'll meet again end of the week to go over particulars. Close the door behind you."

That had been Bob's "Ta", though I doubt he'd ever used such a word.

I hit *save* and the date popped up. Today was March fifteenth: the Ides. How appropriate to return to North Carolina on the unluckiest day of the year. Sullen, I sipped my Fresca and pressed my forehead against the scratched Plexiglas window. The sky had cleared, and with detached foreboding I watched the ground below morph from wedding gown white to lettuce green. My restless mind wandered to places it hadn't visited in a very long time; places it didn't want to go, places of pain and nightmare, of childhood memories. Home.

Rubber found cement, and the plane came to a hurtling stop.

I so don't want to be here...

Acknowledgements

I offer a universe of thanks to my family and friends for their unerring support during this labor of love. My community of readers has served as eyes, ears, psychiatrists, cheerleaders, editors, proofreaders, and sounding board. Thank you critical reviewers: Barbara, Pat, Elaine, and Matt for not gawking as I stood naked on my writing stage, and to Bob Atkinson, whose eagle eyes searched every line of this manuscript for errors and misplaced commas. Thank you Betsy for your snarky technical advice (I don't *care* if Northwestern University doesn't have an undergraduate business school. This is a work of FIC-TION, dammit!), and to Ashley Fontainne of *One of a Kind Covers* for both sage advice and the perfect design.

About the Author

Bestselling Author Virginia Gray is a native North Carolinian and graduate of Wake Forest University. A former college professor, she stepped away from academics to pursue a career in writing. She lives in the

Midwest with her wonderful family and far too many pets.

Made in the USA
Lexington, KY
17 May 2017